PEN PALS:
BOOK TWELVE

LISA'S SECRET

by *Sharon Dennis Wyeth*

A YEARLING BOOK

Published by
Dell Publishing
a division of
Bantam Doubleday Dell Publishing Group, Inc.
666 Fifth Avenue
New York, New York 10103

The trademark Yearling ® is registered in the U.S. Patent and Trademark Office.
ISBN: 0-440-40346-4

Published by arrangement with Parachute Press, Inc.
Printed in the United States of America
August 1990
10 9 8 7 6 5 4 3 2 1
OPM

For "Grandaddy"—Ellsworth Lee Lewis

CHAPTER 1

The clock was just striking twelve as Shanon Davis raced out of Booth Hall and made a dash toward the middle of the quadrangle. She was going to meet her roommate, Lisa McGreevy. For nine whole months, Shanon and Lisa had been roommates in Suite 3-D at the Alma Stephens School for Girls in New Hampshire. They'd become best friends and shared everything, including their mail. Tucked in Shanon's bulging knapsack was an envelope addressed to them both. Shanon knew that Lisa would be thrilled about it, too.

Rounding a curve in the tree-lined walk, Shanon glimpsed a dark-haired girl beneath the clock tower. But it wasn't Lisa; it was Amy IIo, another member of Shanon's suite.

"Hi," Shanon said, coming to a breathless halt. She smiled at Amy. "Where's Lisa?"

"Haven't seen her," Amy replied. The thin, attractive girl ran a hand through her fashionably lopsided haircut. "You two supposed to meet here?"

1

Shanon nodded.

"So are Palmer and I," Amy told her. "As usual, my roommate is making a fashionably late entrance."

Shanon's beautiful hazel eyes gleamed. "Anything interesting in your mailbox?"

"As a matter of fact, I got a letter from John!" Amy said. Opening a guitar case at her feet, she pulled out an envelope. "It's very complimentary," she said. "I guess he's trying to make up for all those notes about the weather."

Shanon took the letter and read it out loud.

Dear Amy,
  What is the opposite of cold? The answer is you. Think of a synonym for extreme that begins with "r"—that's you, too. A metaphor is what's left to my riddle. As the sun is to the earth, I am to you.

Love,
Your pen pal

Shanon chuckled. "Translation, John thinks you're hot, rad, and. . . ." Her voice drifted off as she wondered what the final phrase could possibly mean.

"I can't understand the last part myself," giggled Amy. "I think he means to say that he likes me as much as the planet Earth."

Shanon shook her head. "Whatever it means, you're right—it's certainly complimentary. Got any other mail?" she hinted. "Anything in a small white envelope?"

"There you are!" Before Amy could answer, Palmer Durand joined her suitemates beneath the clock tower. She removed her visor and ran a hand through her golden blond hair. "I distinctly remember that we were supposed to meet at The Tuck Shop," Palmer declared, facing Amy.

"Not true," Amy contradicted. "Before breakfast, we agreed that we'd meet at The Tuck Shop this afternoon. But *after* breakfast, we changed our minds and said we'd meet under the clock. You didn't want to be tempted to buy a milkshake. Remember?"

Palmer frowned. "Oh, right," she murmured in a sheepish voice. "I didn't want to have a milkshake this afternoon because they're so fattening." Dropping the subject, she turned to Shanon and smiled brightly. "Hi!"

"Hi, yourself," Shanon said. "So did you get a milkshake?"

Palmer blushed and looked away. "No, just a small dish of ice cream. I thought as long as I was waiting—"

"Was Lisa at The Tuck Shop?" Shanon cut in.

Palmer shook her head. "Not while I was there."

"We were just discussing the mail," Amy said, fanning her letter from John. "Did you happen to get a note from Sam O'Leary?"

"No," Palmer said with a sigh, "but . . ." she added with a broad smile, "there was something super in my mailbox! It's for both of us!" Whipping a small white envelope out of a notebook, she handed it to Amy.

"What is it?" Amy asked.

Shanon clapped her hands. "I bet I know what it is!"

Miss Palmer Stuyvesant Durand and Miss Amy Elizabeth Ho was written on the envelope in elegant, black script.

Amy gasped. "An invitation!" Her black eyes lit up. "Is it to—"

"Open it and see!" Palmer demanded.

Amy pulled the fine white card out of the envelope and let out a yell. "Wow! They've invited us!"

"Lisa and I got one, too!" cried Shanon. The three girls jumped up and down and giggled.

"I told you it was super news!" said Palmer. She snatched back the invitation and read it out loud. "Miss Maggie Grayson and Mr. Daniel Griffith cordially invite you to the celebration of their marriage to be held on Sunday—"

"I always knew it would happen," Shanon interrupted. "Maggie and Dan were meant for each other! Isn't it romantic? Our two favorite teachers are getting married!"

"It's going to be a great party," Amy said with a nod. "They're holding it in the Meeting House Rose Garden."

"An outdoor wedding is a wonderful idea at this time of the year," Palmer said, tucking the invitation safely away.

"And Miss Grayson is sure to look gorgeous!" said Shanon. "Not to mention Mr. Griffith. . . ." A pink blush crept up her neck.

The girls smiled and exchanged knowing looks. Just about everyone had a crush on their dreamy English teacher, Mr. Griffith. And if anyone was going to have him, it might as well be their trusted dorm counselor and French teacher, Miss Grayson.

The clock chimed a quarter past the hour. "I can't believe it," Shanon said. "Lisa's fifteen minutes late."

"Maybe she forgot," Amy said, shrugging.

4

"We probably got our signals crossed," Shanon reasoned. "Lisa probably got mixed up just like Palmer did. She's probably over at The Tuck Shop this minute, wondering where I am. I'd better get over there. I can't wait to show her our invitation."

Amy eyed Palmer. "I say we go along for the ride. A shake for me and a diet soda for you!"

"I think I can afford to get a shake after all," said Palmer. "It's not as if I'm chubby. I just want to make sure I can wear a bikini this summer."

Rolling her eyes, Amy picked up her guitar case. Shanon slung her bulging knapsack over one shoulder, and Palmer replaced her visor. Then the three girls set off across the quad on their way to The Tuck Shop.

"I'm so excited about being invited to the wedding," Shanon said as they walked along. "When the invitation for Lisa and me came, I was sure that you two had gotten one also."

"Of course all four of us are invited. After all, we are the Foxes of the Third Dimension," Palmer announced. The code name the four girls had given themselves the previous fall when advertising for pen pals at Ardsley Academy, the neighboring boys' school, had stuck.

"I knew from the very beginning that Miss Grayson and Mr. Griffith liked each other," Amy announced.

"It's so wonderful," said Shanon dreamily. "Now they'll live together happily ever after."

Palmer rolled her blue eyes. "We can only hope."

"Just because your parents are divorced doesn't mean that Dan and Maggie are headed for disaster," Amy cut in.

Palmer shrugged. "I hope they stay married forever. All I mean is that their marriage isn't a fairy tale, it's real life."

"Hey, Foxes! High five!" Palmer, Shanon, and Amy ran into another trio from Fox Hall, Gina Hawkins, Kate Majors, and Muffin Talbot. The three newcomers worked on the school newspaper with Shanon.

"Is the meeting of *The Ledger* still on for this evening?" Shanon asked Kate.

"Natch," Kate replied, pushing her glasses up on her nose.

Muffin Talbot, the smallest girl of them all, stepped forward. "We were talking about possible topics for the last issue," she said. "Gina has some great ideas for articles and so does Kate. And I'm just full of plans for the advertising."

"La-dee-da," murmured Palmer.

Catching her expression, Gina clapped Palmer on the back. "What's the matter?" she asked mischievously. "All this shop talk bore you?"

Palmer blushed and smiled at the lovely black girl, admiring her golden brown eyes and wavy black hair. Though Gina was a serious intellectual and Palmer was happy to get a C, the two girls genuinely liked each other. "You could say so. But while you're at it," Palmer added, "I hope the last issue will have some wedding coverage."

Muffin squeaked and drew in a breath. "The wedding! Are you invited? I am!"

"I think everybody in Fox Hall is," volunteered Kate.

"Great," said Amy. "What a bash!"

"Not to mention the number of presents," pointed out Palmer. She glanced at Gina. "Where are you guys going?"

"The Tuck Shop," said Gina. "Upperclassmen get hungry, too."

"Same as us," said Amy. "Let's go. My stomach is growling for that ice-cold shake!"

"I got a pen pal letter from Geordie Randolph," Muffin confided to Amy as the girls continued on their way.

"That's neat," said Amy. "We'll swap. I got one from John."

"Stop by the room tonight, Muffin," Palmer called out. "My latest letter from Sam is ultra cool."

Gina laughed. "Don't tell me you're all still writing to those boys."

"Why not?" Kate called over her shoulder.

"Gina's not into boys," Palmer teased.

Gina gave Palmer a bored look. "You're right," she said, "I'm not. I haven't got time for boys and that's that. Besides, if a boy wrote to me, I wouldn't know what to write back."

The girls burst into good-natured giggles. "I can't believe it," said Palmer. "You're a whole year older than we are. You could be dating one of those cool upperclassmen at Ardsley."

"I'm not interested," Gina protested, "and like I told you, I don't have the time. Besides, boys are so immature. All they know how to do is snow you with smooth lines."

"Not all of them," Shanon protested. "My pen pal, Mars Martinez, is an incredibly honest and nice person. One day you'll meet a boy like him."

Gina looked flustered. "Could we please drop the subject?" she pleaded.

Palmer smiled. "Sure. We didn't mean to make you nervous. It's just that writing to boys is a lot more fun than writing papers."

"Speaking of writing, Muffin said you had some story ideas for *The Ledger*," Shanon said, joining Gina and Palmer. "What did you have in mind?"

"Something to do with current events," Gina replied. "Something international."

Palmer's expression brightened. "What a great idea! How about a preview of the latest fashions for next fall— straight from Paris!"

Gina smiled. "I had someplace like Africa or Asia in mind," she explained. "But I haven't gotten much further than that yet."

"We want the last issue of *The Ledger* to be the best this year," Kate said firmly.

"Sounds exciting," said Shanon. "Can't wait for the meeting."

As the girls approached The Tuck Shop, Shanon picked up her pace and took the lead. "This is really weird," she said, poking her head in the door of the student-run ice-cream bar.

"What's weird?" asked Kate.

"I was sure that Lisa would be here waiting for me," Shanon said, scanning the room.

Kate shrugged. "Maybe she's still in the common room."

"What?" said Shanon in surprise.

"Why would Lisa be in the common room?" Amy asked. "She's coming from art class."

"Lisa wasn't in art class today," said Kate.

"The last time we saw her, she was in Fox Hall, eating a pizza," Muffin piped up.

"See you at the meeting later on," Shanon called out as Gina, Kate, and Muffin headed toward a table.

"What are you going to do?" Amy asked, eyeing the fountain. "You can stay here and have a snack with us."

"No thanks," Shanon said. "I'll go find Lisa."

"I wouldn't," Palmer volunteered. "She stood you up."

"Lisa did *not* stand me up," Shanon declared, feeling her temper rise. Though she was close to Amy and Palmer, Shanon considered Lisa to be her best friend.

"It certainly looks that way to me," Amy said. "Let's face it, Lisa has been acting kind of strange lately."

"She has not," Shanon blurted out. "I mean, she may be a little quiet but—"

"She's downright grouchy," put in Palmer. "This morning, when we were brushing our teeth in the bathroom, Lisa refused to speak to me!"

"People usually don't talk with toothpaste in their mouths," Shanon pointed out.

"Well, are we going to sit down or not?" Palmer asked, finally. "Because if you aren't, I am."

"You two go ahead," Shanon said, forcing a smile. "There must be some sort of mix-up. I wouldn't want to keep Lisa waiting for me."

"Right," said Amy. "Say hello for us—if you find her."

As Palmer and Amy turned away, Shanon tried to maintain her good cheer. She didn't like anyone criticizing her friend, not even the other two Foxes. On the other hand, she had to admit Lisa *had* been acting sort of odd. For the

9

past week and a half, her usually talkative roommate hadn't been herself. Lisa had been sleeping a lot, and putting away extraordinary amounts of food. But Shanon was pretty sure she knew what the problem was. Of all the pen pal relationships in Suite 3-D, Lisa's correspondence with tall, handsome Rob Williams was the most serious. Lisa and Rob thought of themselves as boyfriend and girlfriend. In the course of the school year, Lisa's mood had been affected by trouble with Rob more than once. Though Lisa hadn't yet confided in her, Shanon assumed that her roommate's present moodiness had *something* to do with the fact that the school year would soon be over and that they'd be separated during the summer.

Shanon bought two shakes "to go" at The Tuck Shop and made a mad dash for Fox Hall. Just as Kate had reported, Lisa McGreevy was in the common room. Shanon spotted her best friend's long, silky brown hair over the arm of the couch.

"Hey, Lisa," Shanon announced herself.

Lisa shifted her weight slightly. She was stretched out on the couch as if she'd just eaten a huge meal. At her feet was an empty pizza box.

"Earth to Lisa," Shanon said, coming around to the front of the couch.

"Hi," said Lisa. She propped herself up on her elbow, but didn't look at Shanon.

"Mind if I have a seat?" Shanon asked, trying to keep her tone light.

Lisa sat up and kicked the pizza box off the couch.

"Sure, why not?" she muttered as the box hit the floor with a thud. Shanon squeezed onto the end of the couch.

"I got these at The Tuck Shop," she said, handing Lisa a shake. "I thought you might be there."

"We were supposed to meet under the clock," Lisa said. Shanon's mouth dropped open. "You . . . remembered?"

"Yeah, but I didn't feel like it," Lisa said, gulping loudly. "Thanks for the drink. I'm thirsty."

"Yes, pizza can make you pretty thirsty," Shanon muttered, "especially a whole one. Did you eat that all by yourself?"

"Yes, I ate it all by myself," Lisa mimicked.

Shanon chewed on her straw. She could see that Lisa was in a rotten mood, and she didn't want to add to her misery. But on the other hand, Lisa hadn't met her under the clock and she obviously didn't intend to apologize. . . .

"Are you sick?" Shanon asked.

Lisa gazed at Shanon sadly. "No, I'm not sick," she said quietly.

"Great," Shanon said, trying again to be tactful. "I have something that will cheer you up." She fished the wedding invitation out of her knapsack. Lisa took it and opened it up without a word.

"Isn't it wonderful?" Shanon enthused.

"Great," Lisa said, passing the invitation back. "Did you happen to look in my mailbox?" she asked nervously.

"There was nothing in it," Shanon said. "Why? Are you expecting a letter from Rob?"

Lisa looked bewildered. "Rob? I wasn't thinking about him. I mean, I already got a letter from him this week."

"What did Rob's letter say?" Shanon prodded. "You never showed it to me."

"That's because I haven't had time," Lisa said irritably.

11

She slurped the last of her shake and put down the cup. "I have a lot on my mind."

"I've noticed," Shanon volunteered.

Lisa's brown eyes narrowed. "Noticed what?"

"For one thing . . ." Shanon sputtered, "you're acting weird. Even Palmer says so."

"So now Palmer Durand is talking about me behind my back!" Lisa said angrily.

"No, she wasn't," Shanon protested. "We were just wondering why you didn't meet me and why you didn't speak to Palmer this morning. Kate told us you missed your art class. . . ."

"If there's one thing that really bothers me," Lisa said, "it's people talking about me!"

"But something is bothering you," Shanon argued. "It's Rob, isn't it?"

Lisa took a deep breath. Shanon got the feeling her roommate was about to say something important. But instead, Lisa just turned away.

"Rob is only a boy," Shanon said. "It's silly for you to let some fight you had with him—"

Lisa placed her hands over her ears. "Will you please leave me alone?"

"Okay," Shanon muttered, feeling hurt. For a long time, she stared at Lisa's back. Then her roommate finally turned around. The pained expression on Lisa's face made Shanon feel awful.

"Is—is it something I did?" Shanon ventured.

Lisa shook her head. "That's just like you, Shanon Davis. Just because I'm a little bit upset, you think it's your fault. I just need privacy."

12

"Privacy for what?" Shanon asked softly.

Lisa sighed. "Don't you understand English anymore?" she snapped.

Shanon watched in stunned amazement as her best friend took off up the stairs. Something was definitely bothering Lisa. And whatever it was, it hurt!

CHAPTER 2

"I think everybody in the dorm should chip in for one big gift," Gina suggested, leaning forward on the pink loveseat. Gina, Kate, and Muffin had stopped by Suite 3-D to figure out what to buy Maggie and Dan for their wedding.

"Buying a joint gift takes a lot of organization," Palmer complained. "I don't know if I'm up to it."

"Well, I am," Shanon said eagerly. "I'll even collect the money from everyone."

"I'll help you," Gina volunteered.

"We can break up into groups and scout out the shops in town," Amy suggested.

"If we get a present for Mr. Griffith," Muffin said excitedly, "it'll have to be an antique."

"He does seem to like old-fashioned stuff," Amy said thoughtfully.

"Yes, he does!" Shanon exclaimed. "I'll bet that old desk in his office is an antique."

Kate Majors stood up. "Okay, it's settled. I'll take a poll

14

of the upper-formers for other gift suggestions. They've been here a lot longer than you third-formers," she added, waving a hand at Shanon, Palmer, Amy, and Muffin. "The upper-formers will probably have a better idea about Miss Grayson's taste. After all, she's been the resident faculty person at Fox Hall for a few years now."

Gina and Muffin also stood up to go.

"See you later in the *Ledger* office," said Shanon. "I've got an idea for an article on recycling."

"Sounds good," said Gina. "I'm still trying to think of an article idea with an international theme."

After the trio left, the door to Lisa and Shanon's bedroom opened slowly.

"Are they gone yet?" Lisa asked, sticking her head out.

"Yes," Amy said, "they're gone. Why are you hiding?"

"I'm not hiding," Lisa said. "I just hate crowds. Lately this place has been like Grand Central Station." Crossing the room, she tossed two empty donut boxes into the trash.

"Excuse me," Amy said, clearing her throat, "weren't those *my* donuts?"

"They were in the desk drawer," Lisa said sheepishly.

"I know," said Amy, "and I bought them for all of us."

"What's the problem?" griped Lisa, taking a seat. "They're just a couple of donuts."

"A couple of *dozen* donuts," Palmer remarked, lifting an eyebrow.

Shanon crossed the room and stood next to her roommate. "How was your nap? Do you feel better?"

"I didn't feel bad in the first place," said Lisa, lowering her eyes. "Why are you always accusing me of feeling terrible?"

15

"We have our reasons," Palmer muttered under her breath.

Lisa bent down to lace up her sneakers, ignoring Palmer. "I'm going to the snack bar to cram down some of those dates for history," she mumbled, grabbing a notebook.

"Don't go yet," said Shanon. "The three of us have got letters."

"We were waiting for you to wake up," Amy said gently. "And for Muffin and company to leave."

Lisa's eyes lit up for an instant. "You got a letter from Mars?" she said, smiling at Shanon. "Why didn't you tell me?"

"I was going to," Shanon said eagerly. "We just got back from the mailboxes."

"Nothing for me, I suppose," Lisa said nervously.

Shanon shook her head.

Lisa stared at them earnestly. "And there haven't been any phone messages? Right?"

"Phone messages?" Palmer joked sarcastically. "What are those?"

"The lines on the third floor do make the telephone kind of impossible"—Amy laughed—"not to mention the message-taking system."

Shanon sighed. "We might as well not have one, all right."

"I get the message," Lisa said with a weak smile. "But if there are any calls for me, please let me know."

"Of course we will," Shanon assured her.

"Heard from Rob?" Amy asked.

"Sure," said Lisa. "Sorry I haven't shown you his letter." She went into her bedroom and reappeared with an envelope. "Just put it back on the bureau when you're finished," she added as she slipped out the door.

"Definitely weird," breathed Palmer.

"At least now we'll find out what's on her mind," Amy said, eyeing Rob's letter.

"I was dying to see Rob's letter myself," Shanon said, sitting down beside Amy. "But after Lisa blew up at me because I didn't give her enough privacy I—"

Amy took Rob's letter out of the envelope and started reading it.

"This is great," Amy said. "What's Lisa's problem?"

"Let me see," said Shanon. She read the letter while Palmer peered over her shoulder.

Dear Lisa,

I'm sorry that you've been too busy to write. I miss your letters. Even though my grades haven't been that bad, I'm worrying about finals. I'm scared of the tests. Mainly though, I can't believe that in less than a month we'll be off for the summer. Where will you be? Please write and tell me. I can't wait to see you again. Do you like the beach? I do. More than anything else I'd like to go to the beach this summer with you.

L-O-V-E,
Rob

"He really likes her," Shanon said wistfully.

"I guess she's not having problems with him after all," said Amy. "Except a case of writer's block."

"Let's read our own letters," said Palmer, taking out her letter from Sam. "As usual, it's quite nice," she said, beaming proudly. "Not only that, look at the picture he sent of himself!"

While Amy and Shanon passed around the snapshot of sandy-blond, gray-eyed Sam O'Leary, Palmer reread the letter from her musician pen pal.

Dear Palmer,

It's been a while since we've seen each other so I thought that I'd send you this new picture. As you can see, I've cut my hair short. Even here at Brighton High, the teachers began to think that hair down to my shoulders was a bit much. Not to mention the fact that my mother started mistaking me for my big sister. How's your tennis? Hope we meet again soon. Send me a snapshot if you have one.

Yours,
Sam

"Cute, huh?" said Palmer, taking back Sam's photograph.

"Very cute," agreed Amy. "Listen to my letter from John."

Dear Amy,
   A *is for apple, the very first fruit*
   M *is for muscles, which you have got*
   Y *is for yummy, yak, and yours truly*

Until later,
John

P.S. *The weather has fried my brain, but at least you know I'm thinking of you.*

18

"I think John is running low on material," Palmer said, giggling.

"At least he's thinking of me," Amy sighed. "Let's hear your letter, Shanon."

Shanon picked up Mars's letter. "It's not very long," she said shyly, "but it is . . . kind of personal."

Dear Shanon,

I truly appreciate the recipe for s'mores you sent me and the picture of you and your dog, Sally. I'll add it to my collection. You are out of sight.

Yours truly,
Mars

"Out of sight! That *is* getting personal," Amy quipped.

"I didn't realize your relationship was serious enough to send pet pictures," Palmer said wryly.

Shanon blushed. "Well, Mars likes animals a lot. And Sally is a great dog," she added earnestly. "Any day now she's going to have puppies. I can hardly wait for my mom and dad to call me about it."

Palmer smiled and shook her head. "What about the s'mores recipe? Don't you think that was kind of corny?"

"Mars likes to cook, too," Shanon protested. "And my parents' s'mores recipe is the greatest! Don't knock it till you've tried it."

Palmer rolled her eyes. "I'd love to! Too bad Mars didn't send any samples."

Shanon smiled. "It's a good thing he didn't. You know what chocolate does to my skin. I'd just have to give them to you guys."

"That's the Fox spirit!" said Amy.

A silence fell over the suite. Though the girls had enjoyed sharing their letters, they missed Lisa. Under ordinary circumstances, there would be four of them rolling on the floor with laughter. Since the first semester of school, the Foxes of the Third Dimension had done almost everything together.

"So . . ." Amy ventured, breaking the silence, "we still don't know what's bothering Lisa."

"Rob says in his letter that she's been too busy to write," said Palmer.

"I haven't seen her hitting the books that often," said Amy.

"Lisa has so been studying," Shanon said. "You heard her—she's going over to the snack bar to cram in some history."

"Or to cram in a chocolate sundae," said Palmer.

Palmer began to brush her hair while Amy dropped to the floor to do push-ups.

"We've got to help her," Shanon said, staring out of the window. "It's like we're her family."

Amy sat up. "You're right. The first thing we need to do is to figure out what her problem is. Number one—it's not Rob. Number two—it's not her studies."

"How do you know?" Palmer asked.

"Because Lisa's a good student," said Amy.

"She might be good in a lot of subjects," Shanon said, "but I know for a fact that she got a C on her last math test."

"Only you would get upset about a C," Palmer objected. "No, it's got to be something else." Her eyes fell on the wastepaper basket. "I know what it is!" she cried suddenly. "It's been right under our noses the whole time!"

"What?" asked Amy excitedly.

"Tell us," said Shanon. "It isn't something terrible, is it?"

"Gruesome," said Palmer. "You see those donut boxes in the trash can?"

Amy looked over. "So what?"

"You'll have to agree that Lisa is a lot of things," Palmer continued, "but she isn't a thief."

"Of course she's not a thief," said Shanon angrily. "For heaven's sake, any one of us could have gotten a little hungry and snitched those donuts!"

Palmer put her hands on her hips. "That's not the point!"

"What is?" said Amy.

"If you two haven't noticed," Palmer continued, "Lisa has been pigging out like crazy. This morning at breakfast, she went back for French toast three times. Each plate was loaded with syrup."

"So what?" said Amy. "I like French toast, too."

"Accompanied by two dozen donuts a few hours later?" said Palmer.

"Lisa *has* been eating more than usual," Shanon admitted. "When she ate a whole pizza by herself, I was shocked. She's so thin. Where does she put it?"

Palmer tapped her forehead. "Wait a minute! Is Lisa that thin anymore?"

"Hmmm," said Amy, "she may have put on a few pounds. Actually, we all have."

"More than a few, I think," declared Palmer.

21

"Now that you mention it, she recently gave me a neat-looking pair of pants that she said didn't fit her," said Shanon.

"That proves it," said Palmer. "Lisa is upset because she has an eating problem. For some reason, she's on the road to blimptown and can't stop herself."

"I don't know," said Amy. "Lisa's always had a big appetite."

"And if she had a serious eating problem," Shanon added, "I think I would know about it."

"Would you really?" challenged Palmer. "She hasn't been confiding in you lately, as far as I can see."

Shanon bowed her head. "No, she hasn't. But I think it might be something more serious than food."

"It's not boy trouble," said Amy. "And what other serious stuff could there be? With Miss Grayson and Miss Pryn keeping an eye on everybody, we don't have many opportunities to get into trouble."

"Okay," Shanon said thoughtfully, "suppose Lisa does have a weight problem. What can we do about it?"

"We certainly can't put her on a diet," said Amy. "Lisa isn't the diet type."

"And she'd hate our interfering," Shanon put in. "You know how private she's become."

Palmer pursed her lips. "There's got to be a way, and I think I know what it is. Actually," she added brightly, "this is going to help all of us." Smoothing her blue flowered sun dress, she looked down at her figure. "Yessiree!" she said, sailing out the door. "This is just what all of us need!"

Amy picked up her books. "Where are you going?"

"To the library!" Palmer called over her shoulder.

"Great idea," Amy said. "I've got to study. I wonder what Palmer's got in mind," she said, turning to Shanon.

"I don't know," Shanon said, grabbing her knapsack, "but if it'll help Lisa, I'm willing to try anything."

CHAPTER 3

———◆———

Lisa walked along her favorite path toward the Meeting House Rose Garden. The air was filled with the scent of spring flowers. Ordinarily on a morning like this one, Lisa would have felt as bright as the sunshine. There was nothing she liked more than flowers. But today, not even the hyacinths and jonquils could cheer her up. Nothing could make her happy, not since the letter from her brother, Reggie. . . .

Sitting on a small stone bench, she pulled a crumpled piece of paper out of her skirt pocket. Her big brother's tight handwriting covered the page.

Dear Lisa,

Hey, sis, how are you? What I have to say is a bummer. I went home last weekend and it was pretty awful. Mom and Dad had a big fight. They didn't know that I heard them. Lisa, this is hard to say, but it sounded serious. I just thought I'd warn you—our family may be in for some trouble. But don't tell Mom and Dad that I told you.

How are things at Alma? Finals at Ardsley are killing me. Keep your chin up. If you hear anything, definitely call me. I guess divorce is a pretty common thing these days. Hope we don't join the ranks.

Your brother,
Reggie

Lisa sighed. An ache settled in her throat. For a week and a half, she'd thought of nothing else but her brother's letter. She couldn't believe it—her parents getting divorced! Her legs shook and she broke out into a sweat at the thought of it. She was so horrified by the prospect, she couldn't even cry. And yet she knew that nothing in her life could be more painful. When things were bad, her mother always suggested a big cry. But she felt too numb to do anything.

A soft touch on her shoulder startled her.

"Shanon," she gasped, facing her roommate. "What are you doing here?" She hastily stuffed the letter back into her pocket.

"I—I was just going for a walk," Shanon stammered, looking embarrassed. "Actually, I was looking for you," she added quickly. "I hope you don't mind. I was awake when you sneaked out this morning."

"I didn't sneak out," Lisa protested, her face reddening. "I just wanted some fresh air."

"How about breakfast?" Shanon said cheerfully, remembering her mission. "Palmer and Amy are waiting for us."

"Fine," Lisa said, grabbing her jeans jacket. "I was going to skip breakfast, but on second thought I won't."

"You haven't been skipping too many meals these days,"

25

Shanon said as they started to walk. "I mean, you shouldn't skip meals," she added awkwardly. "That's not very healthy."

Lisa gave Shanon a sidelong look. "What are you talking about?"

"Nothing," Shanon said, flushing. "It's just that good nutrition is an important part of eating."

"I guess so," Lisa said, "but why are you lecturing me about nutrition?"

Shanon giggled uncomfortably. "You'll see. I don't want to ruin the surprise."

Lisa gave Shanon a quizzical look and then dropped the subject. She had more serious things on her mind these days than her eating habits.

"You're wearing your purple denim skirt," Shanon said as they approached the dining hall. "I really like that skirt a lot. It still fits you."

"Of course it fits," Lisa said. "What's that supposed to mean?"

"I only meant that the pants you gave me didn't fit anymore," Shanon hedged, "and I liked those. I like the skirt, too, but I'm still glad it fits you."

Lisa chuckled. "Are you trying to say you want me to give you my purple denim skirt?"

"No," Shanon said, blushing.

"Well, that's what it sounds like," teased Lisa, almost sounding like her old self for a minute. "Anytime you want to borrow it, just say so."

"Thanks," Shanon said, smiling. At least she'd gotten a laugh out of Lisa, even if Lisa hadn't taken the hint about her eating.

Inside the dining-hall entrance, Amy and Palmer were waiting side by side. Palmer was wearing a pink polka-dot dress with matching sneakers, while Amy was dressed in a black skirt and blouse.

"Everything's set," Palmer whispered, grabbing Shanon.

"I spoke to Mrs. Butter," Amy said quietly, using the girls' nickname for Mrs. Worth, the cook.

"What are you whispering about?" Lisa asked.

"You'll see," Palmer said.

"Don't get in line," Amy instructed, steering Lisa to a table set with four trays. "We've got our breakfasts already."

Lisa stood in front of the table and stared at the four bowls of oatmeal. "This isn't what I want for breakfast," she told them.

"Sure you do," said Palmer. "Sit down."

Lisa sat down reluctantly. Beside each bowl of oatmeal was a glass of orange juice and a serving of whole wheat toast. And in the center of the table was a pitcher of milk and a dish of raisins.

"Palmer wanted to put raisins on your oatmeal," Amy said, taking a seat. "But I wouldn't let her."

"Raisins have lots of iron in them," Palmer piped up. "We read about it yesterday in the library."

Lisa looked at Amy and Palmer and then back at Shanon. "I appreciate your getting my breakfast," she said, "but you didn't have to do this. Anyway, how come we're all eating the same thing?"

"Because it's good for us," said Shanon, digging into her oatmeal. "Nutrition is very important. People who don't eat well are irritable."

27

Amy chugged her juice. "That's right. We read all about it."

"Oh, okay," Lisa said with a shrug, "but after the oatmeal, I think I'll have some French toast."

"Oh, no you don't," said Shanon. "French toast is made with eggs."

"Not to mention all that fattening butter and syrup," Palmer said meaningfully.

Lisa looked baffled. "Is someone on a diet?"

"Yes," Palmer blurted out. "You are."

Lisa's eyes popped wide open.

"We, er, we all are," Amy corrected her.

"Actually, we've put together a diet plan," Shanon explained nervously. "I hope you don't mind, but we thought all four of us could benefit." She pulled out a notebook. "See," she said, pointing to a page, "we've planned a menu for the entire week."

"There's an exercise program written down there, too," said Amy.

Lisa sat dumbfounded, listening to her three suitemates.

"Day one is orange juice and oatmeal for breakfast," Palmer explained with a professional air. "We only get to have something gooey on Sunday."

"Where are the pizzas?" Lisa said, scanning the meal plan.

"No pizzas," Amy said staunchly. "No milkshakes or sundaes either."

Lisa shoved the plan away. "No thanks. I've got enough on my mind without thinking about dieting."

"It's not so bad," Palmer argued. "Think about how

you'll look this summer in a swimsuit if you don't watch it now."

"There are all kinds of sports activities planned," Amy added eagerly. "Look, on Wednesday we're all playing tennis together. That'll be fun."

"Even though I can't play tennis," Shanon said. "But I'll try for a good cause," she added.

"Cause?" asked Lisa. "What cause are you talking about?"

"You, of course, silly," said Palmer. "We're only trying to help you—"

Suddenly Lisa pushed her chair away from the table.

"Where are you going?" asked Amy.

Lisa started walking away from the table. "To get some French toast."

"You shouldn't do that," said Palmer. She raced ahead to block Lisa's path.

"You're acting like a nut, Palmer," Lisa said. "Move out of my way."

"You'll be sorry," Palmer said, wagging her finger. "We're only trying to help you. But instead of taking our advice, you're heading for blimptown."

"Blimptown!" said Lisa. "Oh, now I get it," she gasped. "You think that I'm. . . ." She rolled her eyes. "Oh, brother. I thought I had problems. The three of you must have some screws loose. Don't you have anything better to do than meddle in my life?" Turning on her heel, she dashed out the door.

"Wait!" Shanon cried, running after her. Outside, she caught up with her roommate on the sidewalk.

"What's your hurry?" Shanon asked, running to keep up with Lisa.

"I've got English," Lisa muttered without slowing down, "same as you do."

Shanon caught her arm. "Wait up for a minute—"

Lisa stopped and folded her arms. "What is it?"

"We're sorry," said Shanon. "We only wanted to help."

"By putting me on a diet?" said Lisa. "What are you trying to say—that I'm fat?"

"Well, no," said Shanon, "but we all noticed how much you've been eating lately."

"Oh, that," said Lisa, starting to walk again. "When I've got something on my mind, I always eat."

"What about the pants you gave me?" Shanon insisted.

"They were too small when I bought them," Lisa explained.

"Gosh," said Shanon, sounding relieved, "I guess we made a mistake. Palmer was convinced that you had an eating problem."

"She had it all worked out," Lisa said with a soft laugh.

"I think she was interested because of her own figure," Shanon said, giggling.

"Not that I don't have a few extra pounds here and there," Lisa admitted, "but that isn't my problem."

Shanon looked at her seriously. "Please tell me what it is. Maybe I can help."

Lisa turned away. "You don't want to know."

"Yes, I do," Shanon insisted, grabbing her arm. "I'm your best friend. If you can't tell me, who can you tell?"

"Nobody!" Lisa sputtered. "It's too big a secret."

"I get it," Shanon said in a hurt tone of voice. "I guess we're not really friends."

"Of course we are," Lisa said angrily. "It's just that . . ." She wanted so much to confide in someone, especially a close friend like Shanon. But when she thought of what she had to say, the words stuck in her throat. It was almost as if saying it out loud would make it come true. And the thought that her parents might get divorced somehow made her feel ashamed.

"You've been treating me like poison ivy," Shanon lashed out. "If you don't want to be my roommate anymore, just say so! The school year is almost over, anyway."

"I do want to be your roommate," Lisa cried. "It's just that—" Catching the wounded look in Shanon's eyes, a gigantic lump rose in her throat. "I can't talk about it," she choked, turning away. "I'm not even supposed to know about it!"

"Lisa, wait," Shanon called. "I didn't mean to upset you. Come on, let's walk to English together."

"Tell Mr. Griffith I'm sick or something," cried Lisa. As she ran toward the dorm, she saw the campus around her through a haze of tears. The big cry had come.

CHAPTER 4

—————⊂⊃—————

"Listen," Shanon whispered.

Amy and Palmer moved closer to the door of Shanon and Lisa's bedroom.

"Gosh," said Amy, "is she crying?"

"Sounds that way," said Palmer, reaching for the doorknob.

"What are you doing?" whispered Shanon.

"What do you think I'm doing?" replied Palmer. "I'm going inside to find out what's wrong with her."

"She might think we're ganging up on her," Amy said hesitantly. "Maybe we should go get Miss Grayson."

Shanon drew in a breath. "No. I think we need to talk to her first. Even though she acts like she doesn't need us, we may be able to help. And maybe if the three of us go in together, she won't bite our heads off."

Shanon knocked on the door. There was no answer, but they could hear that Lisa's crying had stopped. Palmer opened the door slightly and the three girls peeked in. Lisa sat in the middle of her bed. Her eyes were red and puffy.

Even though it was past ten o'clock, she was still in her nightgown and her dark hair was tousled.

One after another the three girls slipped into the room.

"What are you looking for?" Lisa sniffed, grabbing a tissue.

"You," said Palmer. "You're a mess."

"We heard you crying," Amy said sympathetically.

"I told them you probably wanted privacy," Shanon said, wincing at Lisa's obvious misery.

"It's okay," Lisa said, clearing her throat. "Come on in. I guess I can't keep my secret any longer."

"I hope it's nothing too serious," said Amy.

"Whatever it is, it's affecting all of us," Palmer added.

"I know," Lisa sighed. "I guess I have been hard to deal with lately. It's not because I'm mad at any of you. It's because of this." Reaching for Reggie's letter from under her pillow, she handed it over. Shanon read it first.

"My parents are getting divorced," Lisa announced grimly, getting out of bed. "I've been really worried. I don't know what to do about it."

"Divorced!" breathed Shanon. "How awful!" She passed the letter to Amy.

"It's a bum deal," Amy agreed, bowing her head.

Palmer snatched Reggie's letter away. "Give me that!" She scanned the letter. "I think you should give this another look," she said, tossing Reggie's note on Lisa's bed. "It doesn't say that your parents are getting divorced."

"It does, too!" said Lisa. "If it doesn't happen this month, it's bound to happen sometime real soon. And when it does," she continued, fighting back the tears, "I don't know what I'll do!"

33

Shanon rushed forward to hug her. "Poor Lisa," she cried. "If it happened to my family, I'd feel like dying! I can't think of anything more terrible."

"Don't worry," Lisa said, pulling away. "It'll never happen to you."

"I don't suppose anyone ever thinks it'll happen to them," Amy said quietly.

"Well, I didn't think it would happen to my mom and dad," Palmer piped up. "But it did, and that's that. There's nothing anybody can do to stop it."

"Sorry, I can't be so calm about it," Lisa said, dragging herself to the mirror. "Gosh," she moaned, "my eyes are a mess."

"Come on," Palmer said, "it's a fact of life. Lots of people don't live with both parents. Anyway, you don't even live at home most of the time."

"That's not the point," said Lisa. "Every time I think of it, it hurts."

Palmer lowered her eyes. "It hurt me, too," she said quietly. "I was just trying to cheer you up."

"I know," Lisa said softly.

"After a while, you won't even notice that your parents don't live in the same house," Palmer encouraged. "You'll get two allowances and—"

Lisa stared at Palmer, totally horrified.

"I don't think she cares much about her allowance at the moment," said Shanon. "Is there anything we can do to help?" she asked, touching her roommate's shoulder.

Lisa shook her head "no." "It's just something I've got to get through," she said faintly. "If I can."

"Poor Lisa," whispered Shanon.

"Please, don't do that," said Lisa. "That's one reason I didn't tell you. I don't want everybody feeling sorry for me. Or talking about me, either," she warned.

"You can trust us," said Amy. "We'll keep it a secret."

"As far as I can tell," Palmer pointed out, "there's no secret to keep." She picked up the letter. "All your brother says is that he thinks your family might be in for some problems."

"Palmer's right," said Amy. "Why don't you just call your parents up and ask them what's happening?" she suggested.

Lisa's eyes flew open. "I couldn't do that! First of all, they don't even know that Reggie overheard them fighting. Secondly, what would I say: 'Hi, this is Lisa. Are you guys going to get divorced?' My parents will tell me when they're ready."

"But in the meantime, all you can do is wonder what's really happening," Shanon said with a shake of her head. "It really isn't fair of your parents!"

"Please don't criticize my parents," Lisa said defensively. "They have enough problems."

"Shanon's not insulting your parents," Palmer cut in. "And what she's saying is true. Our parents think they have the right to make decisions that can change our whole lives—sometimes without even telling us! I was really shocked when my dad moved out," she confessed with a sigh. "It would have been better if they'd warned me."

Lisa began to pace the room. "I don't know what to do next," she complained. "School will be over soon and then I'll have to go home and face them. At least I won't be in the dark about everything anymore."

35

"But until then," Shanon said, "we're going to be here to help you."

"I'm really glad," Lisa admitted. "It's been awful not being able to talk to any of you. I wanted to, but I was so confused. Anyway, I didn't want to betray my parents by discussing their personal problems."

Palmer crossed her arms over her chest. "Their problems may not be that bad. I think you should write a letter to your parents today and ask them what's going on."

Lisa cringed. "I couldn't!"

"Then what are you going to do?" said Amy. "From what Reggie says in his letter, your parents had a big fight and that's all there is to it. My parents fight and they're not divorced."

"But mine never fight," argued Lisa. "There's never a cross word between my mom and dad. They're per—" She'd been about to call her parents perfect, but now she didn't know what to think.

"When I met your parents they seemed very happy," reasoned Amy. "Reggie may have misunderstood what he heard."

"If only there was a way you could find out for sure," said Shanon. "Then you'd be able to enjoy the rest of the school year."

"There is a way," Lisa said firmly. She began to get dressed.

"What are you going to do?" Amy asked.

"I'm going to do the same thing that Reggie did," Lisa said, jumping into her jeans. "I'm going to go home and find out for myself what's up."

"When?" asked Palmer.

36

Lisa pulled on a T-shirt. "Now!"

"Now?" gasped Shanon. "You can't possibly do that!"

"Why not?" asked Lisa.

"Be—because," Shanon stammered. "Because of finals, for one thing. You have to study."

"Study—shmudy!" Lisa exclaimed. "I can't study with something like this hanging over my head. At least if I go home and scout out the situation, I'll know how things stand."

"I think going home is a great idea," Palmer said, "but how are you going to manage it?"

"You'll have to ask Miss Grayson," said Amy.

"That's exactly what I'm going to do," said Lisa.

"Isn't there any other way?" Shanon asked nervously. "Going home just before finals seems kind of rash. It's going to be awful around here without you. We'll be really worried."

Lisa smiled gently. "Thanks. But this is something I've got to do. I don't know why I didn't think of it at first," she said, brightening. "As a matter of fact, I feel a lot better already. It's good to get this off my chest," she told them.

"Bet it felt good to cry, too," Amy said, smiling. "I don't cry too often, but when I do I always feel better."

Lisa buckled her belt and pulled back her hair.

"What are you going to tell Miss Grayson?" Shanon asked quietly.

"I'm not sure," Lisa hedged. "If I don't know for sure that my parents are having problems, I'd hate to spread stories that aren't true. Know what I mean?"

"Sure," said Palmer. "And if you tell Miss Grayson what the problem is, she'll tell your parents."

"And they'll know you suspect," volunteered Amy. "You'll have to tell them about Reggie overhearing the argument."

"No," Lisa said thoughtfully, "I don't want to talk to them about that if I don't have to. It would be pretty embarrassing to let your parents know you and your brother had been talking about them behind their backs."

"You'd better make up an excuse," prodded Palmer.

"I don't know," said Amy. "Miss Grayson's pretty smart."

"She's also very understanding," Shanon added. "Maybe you should tell her the truth."

"No," Lisa said quickly, "then I'd have to tell my parents. And if Palmer and Amy are right," she said, brightening, "when I get home, I'll find out that Reggie was making a big deal about nothing."

"Or you'll find out that Reggie was right," chimed in Palmer.

Lisa winced.

"Then what will you do?" asked Shanon.

"I don't know," Lisa replied thoughtfully. "I guess I'll try to talk them out of it."

"How?" asked Shanon. "You have to come back to school."

"Maybe not," Lisa murmured. "The school year's almost over. And if my parents need me."

Amy touched Lisa's shoulder. "What you're going to do isn't going to be easy."

"I know," said Lisa.

There was a knock at the outside door. "Hey—anybody home?" Gina's voice sang out from the front room.

"We're in here," said Palmer.

Gina popped her head into Lisa's room. "Why are the four of you all cooped up in here?" she asked brightly. "Don't tell me," she teased, "you're reading letters from your boy pen pals."

Shanon smiled. "That's not all we do."

"Actually, we were, uh, kind of having a talk," Amy said, glancing at Lisa.

"It's okay," Lisa said softly. "We're just about finished."

"Gee," said Gina, "sorry if I barged in on something. I just wanted to check out an idea with Shanon."

"Sure," Shanon said. "Let's talk in here." She steered Gina into the sitting room.

"What's up?" Gina whispered. "Lisa looks upset."

"We can't talk about it," Shanon said.

Gina nodded. "Well, let me know if I can help," the older girl added. "I just wanted to tell you about this idea I have for—"

"I have an incredible idea for you!" Palmer exclaimed as she joined them.

Gina smiled wryly. "Let me guess. You want a full-page spread on male foreign film stars under the age of fifteen."

"That's not what I was thinking of at all," Palmer stated, turning red. "Though, come to think of it, it's certainly international."

"Palmer does read a lot of movie star magazines," Amy quipped, coming into the room. "And the articles that interest her are most certainly not about women."

"That's not true," countered Palmer. "Anyway, I guess you're not interested in my idea."

"Sure I am," Gina said good-naturedly. "Didn't mean to cut you off."

"What *is* your idea?" Shanon asked curiously.

"To do a big article on boy pen pals," Palmer said excitedly, "only this time they won't be pen pals from Ardsley or even the United States. They'll be pen pals from all over the world! There must be some girls at Alma who would like to have pen pals in Japan or China. Now, if they also happen to be boy pen pals—"

Gina rolled her eyes and tapped her head. "Boys, boys, boys . . ." she said with a giggle. "There are other newsworthy topics in the world."

"It was only an idea," declared Palmer. "Boys aren't poison, you know."

Lisa slipped out of her bedroom, past the sitting-room banter. Ordinarily, she would have found Gina and Palmer's conversation amusing, but at the moment she had too much to think about. She only hoped that Maggie could help her.

When she knocked on the door of the faculty resident's apartment, Miss Grayson appeared holding a long piece of fabric in one hand and a pair of sewing shears in the other. Her reddish-blond curls were pulled up in a casual ponytail. Their dorm counselor looked even younger than usual.

"Hi, Lisa," she mumbled between pursed lips. Shifting the shears to her other hand, she removed a straight pin from her mouth. "That's better. I'm in the middle of re-upholstering this chair. What can I do for you?" Miss Grayson smiled. Her lively face was flushed from the work she'd been doing and her unusual violet eyes were bright with excitement.

"You're busy," Lisa said awkwardly. She glanced around the room. The teacher's usually shipshape apartment was a mess. Stacked on the small oak desk by Maggie's window were piles of books and papers. The floor was littered with scraps of upholstery fabric.

Miss Grayson chuckled. "It looks like chaos, but believe me, I know where everything is." She shut the door behind Lisa. "You'd better sit here," she said, dragging over one of her dining chairs. "Everything else has got something on it."

Lisa smiled. Miss Grayson looked so happy. "I guess you're kind of busy with the wedding plans," she said, reluctant to bring up what was on her mind.

"You could say I'm rather swamped," Miss Grayson replied with a laugh. She dropped the fabric she'd been holding onto the armchair. "Did you and Shanon get your invitation?"

"Yes, we did," Lisa said quietly.

"You don't seem very excited," Miss Grayson teased.

Lisa blushed. "It's not that. . . ." Her voice trailed off, and Lisa began to regret having come at all.

Maggie pulled over the second dining chair and placed it so she could sit facing Lisa. "I'm all yours," she said. "What's up?"

"I need to go home," Lisa burst out.

Maggie cocked her head. "How come?"

"It's, uh, a very private matter." Lisa swallowed hard.

"Can't you fill me in a little bit more?" Maggie said with a hint of firmness. "It's very close to finals. What kind of visit are you talking about? How long a visit are your folks planning?"

"Oh, they don't know anything about it, yet," Lisa explained. "I mean, I want you to call them for me," she added, feeling flustered.

41

"Why can't you call them yourself?" Miss Grayson asked. She searched Lisa's face for an answer. "If you're in some kind of trouble—"

"It's not me," Lisa said hastily, "it's them. I mean—" She bowed her head and sighed. "I want to tell you, Miss Grayson," she continued, "but I'm not sure if there's anything wrong. That's why I have to go home."

Miss Grayson shook her head slowly. "You're not making much sense, Lisa. Is someone sick at home? Is it your grandmother?"

"Oh, no, Gammy's fine," Lisa said, perking up for a moment. "For a month or two Mom had her at home, but she's back at that senior citizens community now. It's not Gammy. . . ."

Miss Grayson looked pensive. "I can see that this is something very private for you," she said, "but if I don't know what the real problem is, how can I help?"

"You can help by calling my mom and dad up," Lisa said in a rush. "Tell them that I've got to go home for a while. Tell them that I'm sick or something."

"I can't do that," Miss Grayson said gently. "I can't lie to your parents."

"Why not?" Lisa burst out. "They're lying to me! They're not telling me what's really going on. And it affects me and Reggie more than anyone!"

Miss Grayson leaned forward. "Are your mom and dad having marital problems?" she asked gently.

A huge lump rose in Lisa's throat. "I don't know," she whispered. "They haven't told me. My brother thinks so. I have to find out, Miss Grayson," she said, struggling to hold back her tears.

Maggie knelt down on the floor and put her arms around Lisa. "Poor girl," she said kindly. "That *is* a very big problem. I'll do what I can."

"Just phone them, please," Lisa begged. "I have to be at home. Just for a week—or even a few days. I promise I'll study for finals. I've got to do something. Please, Miss Grayson. . . ."

CHAPTER 5

Dear Mars,

It's the middle of the night and I can't sleep. Lisa is all bundled up in her covers. I'm writing with my flashlight. Maybe I can't sleep because it's so hot. The window is open and no wind is getting through. I feel bad. I think that's the real reason. Also, Lisa is having a rough time and that makes me feel bad, too. It's a private matter. At first she didn't even tell me what was wrong, but now I know. But I can't tell you because she made us all promise to keep it a secret.

Anyway, Lisa's trouble affected us all. When she didn't tell me what was on her mind, I thought maybe she was acting funny because she didn't like me anymore. But now I know that's not true. Anyway, Lisa is going home and I'm going to miss her. Nine months is a long time to live with someone who's not in your family. You get to know a lot about them. Like I know that Lisa has a temper but she doesn't really mean it when she gets angry. I'm so lucky to have her as a roommate.

Sorry I can't talk about much but Lisa, but she's on my mind. From the very beginning, we had so much in common. Palmer and Amy had a lot of problems arranging their room, but Lisa and I didn't. We even agreed right away what to put up on the walls. We bought a poster together with big sunflowers on it. It's kind of worn out now at the edges. I'm afraid you may think this letter is boring. I wish we were in the same room so we could talk. But at least writing has made me sleepy.

How is your studying for finals going? Are you looking forward to the summer? I'm going to be working in my father's garage—this time at the gas pump instead of in the convenience store. Mom and Dad are taking us all camping for a few weeks in August. I'm excited about it. We have two big five-man tents that we set up on some land we own in the mountains. Someday when we save enough money, my dad is going to build a cabin for us to stay in during the summer. He's been talking about this for a long time. What do you do in the summer with your parents? Sorry, but parents are on my mind. If something happened to my mom and dad to make them break up, I don't think I could stand it. Do your mom and dad get along well? Please write me soon. I'm glad you like the picture of Sally. I'll let you know when she has pups. My mom and dad are going to do a home delivery like usual. Your last letter was very complimentary. I like you.

Yours truly,
Shanon

P.S. Please do not tell Rob that Lisa is going home. It is her choice if she wants to tell him.

P.P.S. *A piece of exciting news is that Maggie and Dan, our French and English teachers, are getting married and the whole dorm is invited to the wedding! It's going to be held outdoors. If you have any great ideas for a present, please write me. We are each chipping in two dollars to get a big one. At the moment, we are thinking about something antique.*

P.P.P.S. *The last issue of* The Ledger *is going to be pretty innovative. We have this idea of tying in current events more to open up the paper to the outside world. I'm doing an article tying in Alma with environmental issues. Kate is trying to interview the mayor, and Gina is trying to think of something international to write about. (I'm going to bed now.)*

The sky was overcast on the day that Miss Grayson drove Lisa into town to the train station. Shanon, Palmer, and Amy came along, too. In the very back of the van were Kate and Gina. After Lisa was dropped off, the girls had made a plan to go shopping. There wasn't much talk among the members of Suite 3-D during the ride into town. Gina and Kate, unaware of Lisa's reason for leaving, were in high spirits.

"So, let's hear it from our foreign correspondent, Gina Hawkins," ribbed Kate, "on location in the Canary Islands."

"Very funny," Gina said, laughing. "I only wish that I could be a traveling journalist one day."

"Where would you go?" Kate asked.

"Maybe the Soviet Union or Poland," Gina replied. "I'd

46

like to interview people our age and see what life is like from their point of view."

"Good luck," said Kate. "As for me," she boasted, "I've already got an interview date with the mayor." Leaning forward in the car seat, she tapped the back of Shanon's shoulder. "How are you doing on the environmental story?" she asked.

"I haven't started it yet," Shanon replied dully. At the moment, *The Ledger* issue was the last thing on her mind. The only thing she could think about was Lisa's leaving.

"Here we are," Miss Grayson said, pulling into the train station parking lot. Lisa opened the front door and grabbed her fat suitcase.

"Let me get that for you," Shanon said, squeezing past Amy and Palmer. By the time she'd hopped out, Lisa was already walking toward the tracks.

"Hey, wait for us," Shanon said. She ran after Lisa with Amy and Palmer.

"I'll go check and see if the train's on schedule," Miss Grayson said, heading for the office.

Gina and Kate both waved from the car. "See you, Lisa!" cried Gina.

"Have fun at home!" called Kate.

Lisa set down her suitcase next to the track. Amy put a hand on her shoulder. "Hang in there," she said. "If you need us, send an SOS. We'll hire a balloon to take us to Pennsylvania."

"Yes, keep in touch," Palmer said. "Things are going to be okay however they work out." She forced a smile. "My parents broke up and look at me."

47

"Yes, look at you," Amy joked, rolling her eyes.

Lisa giggled uneasily and Shanon moved closer to her friend. "Be sure to write," Shanon said, giving Lisa's hand a squeeze. "I'll be thinking about you."

"I'll be thinking about you, too," Lisa said, squeezing Shanon's hand back.

"Make sure you come back soon," Shanon added wistfully.

Lisa smiled and looked at Shanon's face. Her roommate's eyes were swimming with tears. "I'll miss you!" she said, choking up at the sight of Shanon about to cry.

"I'll miss you, too," Shanon said softly.

"Okay, Foxes! How about a big sandwich?" Amy suggested.

"A Lisa sandwich!" squealed Palmer. Feeling the three girls all hug her at once, Lisa laughed.

"The train's on time," Miss Grayson announced. She kissed Lisa's cheek. "Give your parents my regards," she said. "I think we've got your mom pretty baffled by this visit."

"That's the way I want it," said Lisa stubbornly.

"Phone if you need advice," said Maggie.

"Don't worry," said Lisa. "I can handle it. And, Miss Grayson . . . thanks!"

The train pulled up at the station. It would take her to Boston, where she would catch a flight to Pennsylvania at the airport. Lisa picked up her suitcase and began boarding the train.

"Do you have everything?" Amy cried out over the screeching whistle.

Lisa nodded.

"What about your airplane ticket?" Shanon yelled.

Lisa shook her head again and grinned. "It's in my suitcase!"

From the porch of the small station house, Shanon, Amy, and Palmer watched as the train pulled out. "She's going to be okay," Amy said quietly.

"Sure she will," said Palmer.

"I hope so," Shanon said. "There's nobody in the world like Lisa."

"Let's split up," Kate directed. "That way we can hit more stores." Having seen Lisa off at the station, the girls stood in the Brighton town square. Miss Grayson had given them forty-five minutes for shopping.

"I think splitting up is a good idea," Palmer agreed. "I'll check out the antique store down by the mall."

"Great," said Kate. "It's called Miller's Antiques."

"Isn't that across from the Brighton Pharmacy?" said Gina. "This could be tricky. That's where Miss Grayson said she was going."

"There are two antique stores," pointed out Shanon. "One's nowhere near the pharmacy."

"I think we should check out both of them," Palmer said stubbornly. "And I'll check out the one in the mall."

"Hey, wait a minute," Amy said with a giggle. "The pharmacy isn't the only place across from Miller's Antiques. It's also across from Suzy's Shoe Emporium."

"So what?" said Palmer with a blush.

Amy chuckled. "Suzy's Shoe Emporium is where Sam

49

works on the weekends—that's what," she teased.

"Is there a law that says I can't see my pen pal?" Palmer said. "If I happen to be going to a store right across the street from Suzy's—"

"Less talk, more action," snapped Kate. "If we don't get going, Miss Grayson will be back here and we won't have bought anything."

"You're right," said Shanon. "I'll go to the antique store that's near the farmers' market."

"I'll go with you," said Amy.

"I'm going to check out George's Flea Market," said Kate. "And by the way, Amy, why are you lugging your guitar around with you?"

Amy smiled mischievously. "You never know—I might get inspired to make a public appearance."

Kate rolled her eyes. "Well, just remember that we're on a serious mission here. We don't get into town all that often. Come on, let's move it!"

Palmer looked at Gina. "That leaves us two."

"Okay," said Gina. "I'm with you."

The girls fanned out. "Let's meet back here in twenty minutes," Kate yelled over her shoulder.

Palmer and Gina headed down Main Street. Passing by the windows of the quaint stores in Brighton's historic district, the two girls caught sight of their reflections. Palmer was wearing a rust blazer with a white blouse and a pleated plaid skirt. Her long hair was pulled back with a tortoiseshell barrette that matched her horn-rimmed glasses. She'd taken off her hat so she could fully enjoy the sunshine. Gina was wearing a green cotton sweater and a black denim skirt. Her red leather belt matched her boots and red paisley scarf, and in one of her ears was an earring.

"Where'd you get that earring?" Palmer asked, eyeing the long, dangling piece of jewelry in Gina's ear. The clay earring was molded in the shape of a dark-haired girl in red boots.

"My friend at home made it for me," said Gina, smiling. "I think it's supposed to be me."

Palmer giggled and looked at Gina's feet. "The girl on the earring has on red boots. The same as you do."

"These are my favorite boots," Gina admitted. "I've been wearing them forever."

"Not me," said Palmer. "I try to wear a different pair of shoes every day. Of course, I don't have *that* many pairs. But I can do it for about two weeks."

"Wow," said Gina, "that's impressive. No wonder you picked a boyfriend who works in a shoe store."

"Oh, that's not the reason," Palmer said in surprise. "Sam's got more than that going for him. Wait until you see!"

"I can't wait," Gina said, smiling.

Palmer glanced at the older girl's profile. Gina was someone she'd always looked up to, but their taste could not have been more different. Palmer would never have worn red boots or the red paisley scarf that Gina was wearing. And she wouldn't be caught dead wearing only one earring. But on Gina, these original touches looked great. Palmer was glad that she had the opportunity to become friends with Gina. She'd never been all that close to a

51

black girl before.

"Here we are," Gina announced, stopping in front of the antique store.

Palmer stared hungrily at the shoe store across the street. "I wonder if Miss Grayson is still in the pharmacy," she hinted.

"Why don't you check it out?" Gina said with a giggle. "After that you could pop into the shoe store."

Palmer smiled gratefully. "Thanks. I won't be a minute. Come and get me if you find anything interesting."

As Gina climbed the stairs to the antique store, Palmer darted across the street to the pharmacy. Taking a quick glance inside, she saw that Miss Grayson wasn't there. She made a beeline to Suzy's Shoe Emporium. Smoothing her dress as she sailed in, she tried to look casual. She was sure that Sam would be there since he worked at the emporium on Saturdays. But instead of Sam, the salesperson was a young woman.

"Can I help you?" she asked.

Palmer's face turned pink. For some reason she felt embarrassed. "Uh, I'm just looking around," she muttered, shifting a pair of tan shoes. She wondered if Sam was working in the back.

"Is there anything in particular you'd like to see?" the girl asked, sticking close by.

"Actually," Palmer said, clearing her throat, "I'm looking for someone who works here. Sam O'Leary."

The salesperson smiled. "I guess a lot of people are looking for Sam. He and his band have been getting a lot of publicity lately."

"Yes," Palmer said, beaming. "I'm a friend of his. Is he around? Just tell him it's Palmer."

"Sam's not here today," the girl said.

"Thanks anyway," Palmer said, barely able to cover her disappointment. Turning toward the door, she nearly bumped into Gina as she entered the store.

"No luck," sighed Palmer. "Sam's not here."

"Too bad," said Gina. "I found something in Miller's—a bird print of a raven. I think it's an Audubon!" she added excitedly. "I'll meet you there in a minute. There are some hiking boots here that I—"

"Yuk!" muttered Palmer. "Hiking boots. See you later."

As the door shut with a jingle behind Palmer, Gina rushed over to the display near the window. Hiking boots were just what she'd been looking for. She reached for a boot to examine it more closely.

"Excuse me," a boy's voice said, "I was looking at those."

Gina turned. A handsome dark-skinned boy was smiling at her.

"I might buy them," he explained. His dark eyes had a mischievous look. "I was in here last month. They said these shoes were on order."

"I think they're girls' boots," Gina said firmly.

"I'm considering them for my sister," the boy explained. "This may be the only pair in her size in the store."

"I'm afraid that is the last pair in that size," the salesperson said, walking over.

Gina let go of the shoes and walked away. "Okay, I

guess they're yours. I'm in too much of a hurry to try them on, anyway."

The boy tapped her shoulder. "I have an idea!"

Gina turned around in surprise. "What is it?" she asked.

"Since you and my sister wear the same size boot, perhaps you'll do me the favor of trying them on?" he suggested politely.

Gina blushed. "Okay," she said impulsively. "Your sister must have big feet," she added with an embarrassed giggle.

The boy's smile became a grin. "She does."

"I'll try them on," Gina agreed, "but I have to hurry."

"I really appreciate it," the boy said, sitting down next to her.

Gina whipped off one of her short red boots and plunged her foot into the heavy hiking boot, meanwhile keeping an eye on the window for Palmer.

"They're good-looking boots," the boy said cheerfully.

"Thanks," Gina said, feeling slightly embarrassed. She wasn't used to boys staring at her feet, especially ones with such great smiles.

"Where are you going hiking?" he asked, leaning forward.

"The Adirondacks," she mumbled, taking the boot off. "Where are you going?" she asked.

"I hope we are going to South Africa this summer," the boy said.

"South Africa?" said Gina, in surprise. "Why there?" South Africa was in the papers a lot these days, but she'd never heard of anybody going on a vacation there.

"South Africa is my home," the boy told her.

"Wow," said Gina, "that's interesting. I've never met anyone from South Africa before. What's your name?"

"Themba," said the boy, just as the door jingled loudly.

"Come on!" yelled Palmer. "The bird print is terrible, but I did find some antique earrings for myself!"

"Antique earrings?" Gina laughed. "Oh, brother!"

"Let's go," Palmer urged her. "I want to stop in Brighton Sports—"

"I have to leave," Gina told Themba. Flustered, she quickly put her red boot back on.

"How are the boots?" the boy asked, standing up.

"Not great, actually," Gina admitted. She stood up and hurried out. "Good-bye," she called over her shoulder. "I'm sorry, but I have to get back to my friends."

"Good-bye," the boy called in reply. "Until we meet again!

"Shanon, Amy, and Kate are going to be wondering what happened to us," Gina said when she joined Palmer outside. She and Palmer began hurrying down the block.

"I guess I lost track of the time," said Palmer.

"In any case," Gina said, "we can't stop in Brighton Sports. I think we should go to George's Flea Market."

"All right," Palmer agreed breathlessly. "I just wanted to check out the summer stuff, but I'll do that next time."

The two girls started to jog. Gina smiled and glanced over at Palmer. "Nice earrings," she commented.

"Thanks," Palmer said, enjoying the feel of the long,

dangling crystals. "They're long like yours are," she added breathlessly. "Who was that boy in the store? A friend?"

Gina blushed. "No, I just met him. He's from South Africa."

"Gee," said Palmer, slowing down, "that's a long way from here. What's he doing in Brighton, New Hampshire?"

"I wish I'd had a chance to ask him," Gina said.

Palmer smiled mischievously. "Sorry I rushed you. He looked like he was about our age."

"Probably," Gina said.

"He was cute, too," said Palmer. "What was his name?"

"Themba," Gina replied. "He seemed very interesting."

The girls stopped to look in a store window.

"Don't tell me you think a boy is interesting?" teased Palmer. She smiled at Gina's reflection in the glass.

"I'm sure that some boys are," Gina said stiffly.

"Come on," Palmer said with a giggle. "I bet if you got to know somebody like—"

Gina laughed in spite of herself. "Cut it out. Anyway, I'll never see him again. He's not from here, remember?"

"He might be staying here with someone," Palmer said brightly. "You could find out."

"No thanks," said Gina. "Nancy Drew I'm not."

"Whatever you say," Palmer said.

Gina grabbed Palmer's hand. "Come on, let's get going!"

"Okay," Palmer said, running to catch up with her friend. "I think you're the craziest person I've ever known in my life," she confessed with a giggle.

"Same here." Gina laughed. "Sometimes I wonder why—"

"Why what?" Palmer panted.

Gina winked. "Why . . . I like you so much!"

CHAPTER 6

Dear Lisa,

We thought we'd do a drawing of ourselves to let you know exactly what's going on in your absence. First, here is the explanation of the picture. The figure on the left is Palmer. We managed to get into town to look for Maggie and Dan's wedding present, after we dropped you off, and Palmer ended up buying earrings for herself! I think Gina's funky earrings gave her the idea.

It feels like years instead of weeks are left to the term when I look at the ton of work I've got to do. Even Palmer is beginning to get worried. This morning Amy had dark circles under her eyes from staying up too late working on

Latin. She is entering some national contest next week. However, this does not *prevent her from doing what you see in the last picture. That's right, she's playing her guitar in the town square! I was so proud of her. A lot of people stopped to listen, including Maggie, which made it even harder for us to shop for her wedding gift. I think Amy got the idea from Sam O'Leary, who sings in the square sometimes with his band. How is the weather in Pennsylvania? Here, it feels like summer. All I want to do is eat ice-cream cones. As you can see in the middle of the picture, I am still working hard on* The Ledger *and I think my idea for an article on recycling is very good. I went to the recycling center and learned about all the new procedures. I was surprised to learn that many things are not recyclable! Instead of finding pots and musical instruments like archaeologists did when they unearthed Pompeii, which was covered by a volcanic eruption all those centuries ago, people will remember us by big plastic cartons.*

We are all hanging in, Lise. But we miss you. I want to ask you about your mom and dad, but I also want to respect your privacy. If what is happening to you was happening to me, though, I probably wouldn't be able to stop talking about it. Anyway, I was glad you decided to tell us in the end. We'd like to know how you are, so please write us a letter. And hurry back! You wouldn't want to miss finals!

> *Love,*
> *Shanon*

Dear Sam,
  How are you? I am fine. I was in Brighton this weekend.

59

I stopped at Suzy's Shoe Emporium, but the salesperson (who was a girl) said you weren't there. She seemed to be a fan of yours. It's a shame you weren't around. Amy did some singing out on the square. It was great. What's new? With me it's the same old thing—too much studying and not enough fun. I liked your last picture. I wanted to ask you if you knew a boy named Tim Bay from South Africa. This friend of mine met him in town and thought he seemed very interesting. Have you ever met Gina Hawkins? She's the one who wrote the school play and she also writes articles for The Ledger. *She's your age. She's very different from me, but we're getting to be good friends. She likes The Dead and wears tie-dye, plus she's an intellektual (sp?). Gina is a lot of fun. Write to me soon. How are your friends at school? I wish I knew more of them.*

Yours,
Palmer

Dear Shanon,

I got your last letter. You sounded very sad. I hope you are getting along without Lisa. I know how I'd feel if Rob or John took off. I'm used to the guys, though I could do without some of their bizarre habits. (Rob chews his toenails. Do not tell Lisa.) Speaking of my ace Rob, he is not happy, I repeat, not happy that Lisa has stopped writing. He really cares about her. Could you do something to help him out? How come Lisa can't tell him what's going on with her? He was shocked when I told him she'd gone

60

home. I think he might call her if she doesn't write to him soon. Sorry, but I had to tell him that she wasn't at school. He's been writing her letters all year and I think he has the right to know. Hope you're not mad at me.

Sincerely,
Mars

Dear Mars,

I will try to get Lisa to write Rob. Of course I'm not mad at you! I just hope Lisa isn't mad at me when she finds out that Rob knows where she is.

Love,
Shanon

Dear John,

I'm sorry I haven't written to you in a long time. Your last poem is kind of hard to understand, but I take it as a compliment. What are you doing these days? I sang in the town square at Brighton.

Yours truly,
Amy

Dear Amy,

Wish I had caught you singing in town. I've been cramming these days myself. Have you heard how well our soccer team is doing? Ardsley has come out of the woodwork! The team has practices on Saturdays at three on the big field. I saw some Alma and Brier Hall girls in the bleachers. Anyway, if you have some free time, why don't you and the other Foxes come over this Saturday. The

61

Unknown (Mars, Rob, and I still call ourselves that) will be there waiting. I tried a little harder on this poem. Hope you didn't mind that in the last poem I said you had muscles. It was meant as a compliment.

> Thinking of you
> In the solemn castle of my noodle
> Grinding out those grades
> Energized by bars of chocolate
> Rays will soon be the rage
Can't keep my mind off summer.

Yours,
John

Dear Lisa,

Did you get our letter with the drawing? I hope you get it before you return to Alma! I'm sorry to tell you that Mars spilled the beans to Rob that you're at home. Hope this is okay with you. Rob would probably appreciate hearing from you.

Love,
Shanon

Dear Shanon, Amy, and Palmer,

You cannot believe how great it is to be home. (Of course, a day doesn't go by that I don't miss the Foxes.) My parents have been absolutely super! Mom took me shopping and bought me two new dresses, and Dad has driven me to the mall a hundred times! We've been out to dinner twice! I've tried to study a couple of times, but I just can't seem to concentrate. It's like a holiday and my parents are treating me like I'm a celebrity. Sometimes they *seem to be a little quiet, but I'm sure that's normal. I certainly haven't heard any big fights! I didn't even have to tell them why I came home. Of course they were very worried about me, since Maggie told them I had something urgent to discuss with them and that I was very unhappy. But all I did was tell my parents that I was homesick, and they believed me! I feel kind of guilty about lying, but it's for a good cause. Sometimes when I'm alone—which isn't too often since my parents are so busy trying to cheer me up—I think about the nutrition plan you three cooked up. It was very funny that you thought my problem was chub! (Soon it's going to be bad grades if I don't crack those books!) But your plan looked great, anyway! So, I'm glad to report that I am very, very happy. In spite of his being a genius, my brother, Reggie, isn't so smart after all! I will be back soon, maybe before you get this letter.*

Love and XXX's!
Lisa

CHAPTER 7

—————◆—————

"All aboard who's coming aboard!" Mr. Griffith yelled good-naturedly.

"This is really, really nice of you to drive us to Brighton," Shanon bubbled, squeezing into the back of the car with Amy and Palmer. "Two Saturdays in a row, now that's a treat!" Gina, who had come along too, had taken the seat up front next to their teacher.

"What's the first stop?" Mr. Griffith asked. "Figaro's or Lulu's Diner?"

The girls burst into giggles at the mention of the small town's favorite teen hangouts.

"Actually, I want to check out Suzy's," Gina announced.

"My favorite spot!" Palmer squealed. "How come you want to go back? Don't tell me you're actually going to buy those hiking boots."

"I lost my red paisley scarf last weekend. I finally remembered that the shoe store was the last place where I was wearing it," said Gina.

"Maybe Sam found it for you!" Palmer suggested.

"Okay, Suzy's Shoe Emporium for Gina and Palmer," said Mr. Griffith as he pulled out of the campus parking lot, "and I have to go to the copy shop, the florist, the jeweler—"

"The jeweler?" Amy said, giggling. "Why are you going to go there?"

Mr. Griffith cleared his throat. "Rings!"

The girls laughed in unison. "Can we go with you and see?" begged Palmer.

"Not until the big day," warned Dan. "Now, tell me what other errands you girls have to run."

Palmer, Amy, and Shanon gave each other knowing looks. "Oh, we just want to wander around," Shanon said casually. "But before we go to soccer practice at Ardsley, I do have one other important stop."

Mr. Griffith eyed her in the rearview mirror. "What's that?"

"Home," Shanon said, blushing. "My folks live right off Mulberry Avenue."

"How come you want to go home?" Gina asked, turning around in the front seat.

"I want to see Sally," Shanon said shyly.

"Shanon's dog had pups," Amy explained, loud enough for Mr. Griffith to hear. "We thought we'd go see them."

"Sure," Mr. Griffith said, turning a corner. "I'd be interested, too. I love animals." Pulling up at a meter, their teacher parked the car and everyone got out.

"We'll meet here at one-fifteen," Mr. Griffith announced, checking his watch. He put some coins in the meter. "That'll give us enough time to buzz by Shanon's house before heading over to Ardsley."

"Okay, Mr. Griffith," said Amy.

Palmer smiled and waved. "We won't be late. We promise."

Mr. Griffith smiled and walked away.

"Thanks a lot!" Shanon called after him.

"Keep an eye on them, Gina!" Mr. Griffith said, looking over his shoulder.

"Don't worry, Mr. Griffith," Gina replied, "I will!"

The girls stood in a spirited huddle. "Where do we go first?" asked Amy excitedly.

"We haven't got much time," Shanon said, darting a look at the big clock. "Since we've all got to check everything out, I think we should stick together."

"Okay," said Palmer, "let's go to the Shoe Emporium."

"Just a minute," Amy said, grabbing her elbow. "We're not going to find a wedding gift there. I thought you were just kidding about going to Suzy's."

"Gina needs to look for her scarf," argued Palmer.

"That part is true," Gina admitted. "I'll just stop in for a minute when we go to Miller's Antiques. That's one of the stores on the list." She pulled out a piece of paper. "In Miller's Antiques, Kate saw an old-fashioned punch bowl set; in George's Flea Market, Kate says there's a wrought-iron dog that we should check out; in Plain 'n' Fancy, Kate says that there's an embroidered table cover—"

"What is this?" Amy asked. "If Kate thinks this stuff is so great, why isn't she here?"

"She has her interview with the mayor's office today," Shanon reminded her. "After Kate scouted out all these gift possibilities, the least we can do is look at them. Dolores and Muffin suggested some things that they saw, too."

"Let's get started," said Gina, taking off down the street. "If each of us takes a quick look at the suggestions—"

"Where are we going?" asked Shanon, running up alongside of Gina.

Gina smiled at Palmer. "First stop, Miller's Antiques!"

Palmer beamed. "And Suzy's Shoe Emporium!"

The group reached the mall and went into Miller's. "I say it's a nerdy choice," Palmer said, taking one look at the punch bowl.

"I don't know," Shanon disagreed. "My mom and dad have a punch bowl that they use a lot, especially on holidays."

Palmer shrugged and glanced at the door.

"Why don't you go to Suzy's while we're deciding," said Gina.

Palmer lunged for the door.

"And don't forget to ask about Gina's scarf," Amy called after her.

Once she was outside, Palmer caught her breath. Instead of running, she walked slowly across the street. If Sam was in today, he'd be able to see her coming toward the store. She didn't want him to think she was dying to see him. Smoothing her pink dress, she ambled up to the store. Sam O'Leary's handsome face appeared at the window.

"Hi," he said, eagerly opening the door. His smile was dazzling.

"Oh, Sam . . . hi," she said, trying hard to sound as if she hadn't expected to see him. "I was across the street in Miller's Antiques and I thought I'd stop by."

"Why are you staring?" Sam asked.

"I'm just glad to see you," Palmer said, turning red. "I didn't realize I was doing that."

Sam turned and looked in the mirror. "Good. For a moment I thought you saw my chicken pox."

Palmer's mouth dropped open. "Chicken pox!" Moving closer, she detected a few faint, pink marks on Sam's face. "Are you still sick?" she whispered.

Sam chuckled. "It's okay, I'm not contagious. I *had* the chicken pox. I just have a few spots left over."

"Is that why you weren't working last weekend?" Palmer asked sympathetically.

"Yes," replied Sam. "It's kind of embarrassing at my age."

"You don't have to be embarrassed with me," said Palmer. "I had poison ivy last summer. And even if you were contagious it wouldn't matter to me. I had chicken pox when I was six, and I don't think you can catch—"

Gina hurried into the shop. "Did you get it?" she asked.

"Get what?" Palmer asked, looking at Gina blankly.

Gina smiled. "The scarf. Remember? Did you ask about it?"

"Oh, gosh," Palmer said sheepishly. "I'm sorry. I—"

"It's okay," Gina said with a giggle. "Hi, I'm Gina," she said, turning to Sam. "I think I may have left a red paisley scarf here. Kind of wild-looking. Have you seen it?"

"Nobody's turned it in," Sam said, checking behind the counter. "If they do"—his face lit up suddenly—"so *you're* Gina! Palmer mentioned you in a letter."

"She did?" Gina said, looking pleased.

Sam came out from behind the counter. "I'm sorry that I didn't know Tim."

Gina frowned. "Tim?"

Sticking her head in the store, Shanon announced, "Amy and I are going to George's Flea Market to check out the dog! No go on the punch bowl!"

"Okay," Gina said, "we'll catch up with you later!"

"We're trying to find a wedding present for our teachers," Palmer explained to Sam.

"Yes, and we're sort of in a hurry," Gina said.

"All right, we'll leave," Palmer sighed. "Great to see you, Sam," she said to her pen pal. "I've got to get going."

"Great to see you, Palmer," said Sam. "If I run into anybody from South Africa called Tim Bay, I'll let you know," he told them.

When she left the shoe store, Palmer felt as if she were floating on air instead of walking on cobblestones. "I can't believe how lucky that was!" she said. "He was all alone with no customers! How about a quick stop at Brighton Sports?"

"Absolutely not," Gina snapped. "We've already made one stop too many because of you."

"Because of *your* scarf," Palmer reminded her.

Gina sighed. "Yeah, it's too bad about that. I got that scarf from my mother. Anyway, what in the world were you thinking of a minute ago?"

Palmer stared at her friend. "What do you mean?"

"Why were you and Sam talking about Themba?" asked Gina.

"I just asked Sam in a letter if he knew a boy from South Africa called Tim Bay," said Palmer.

"How could you do that without asking me first?" Gina

protested. "Besides, his name is Themba, not Tim Bay!"

Walking rapidly, the two girls had almost caught up with Amy and Shanon.

"I thought I could help. You seemed interested in him," Palmer explained. "What's the big deal?"

Gina glared at Palmer in frustration. "I don't even know him! How can I be interested in him?"

"I can't believe that a girl as sensible as you is scared of boys," Palmer challenged.

"I am not," Gina argued as they approached George's Flea Market. "Just because I happen to say a few words to a boy in a shoe store doesn't mean I want you to fix me up with him!" She shook her head and climbed the stairs quickly to catch up with Amy and Shanon.

Palmer reddened and stopped at the door. "And just because I asked Sam if he knew Tim—I mean, Themba—doesn't mean that I was trying to fix you up," she said firmly. "You said that you thought Themba's background was interesting, remember? You called him 'international.' Since you were interested in writing about something international for *The Ledger*—"

"You thought I might want to interview him?" Gina guessed.

Palmer nodded.

"Gee," she said, "I hadn't thought of it, but thanks for looking out for me," she said, smiling. "You're full of surprises, Palmer."

"Remember that the next time I do something without asking you first," said Palmer.

"What are you two waiting for?" Shanon demanded,

sticking her head out the door. "Come and see this wrought-iron dog. It's neat!"

"Arf, arf," Amy joked, appearing in the window with the dog.

"I've never seen anything more gross in my life," whispered Palmer.

Gina motioned for Amy to join them outside. "Next stop—Plain 'n' Fancy," she said, taking out the list.

Shanon groaned. "If only Lisa were here. . . ."

"Lisa *does* have good ideas," agreed Amy.

"At the rate we're going, we'll never get a present," griped Palmer. "If all the ideas on the list are this bad, we're in deep trouble."

When the girls finally got back to the car, Mr. Griffith was waiting.

"Did you finish all your errands? Where are your packages?" he asked gaily.

Amy sighed. "We didn't have much luck. . . ."

"It can't be that bad," he said. "Hop in! Next stop—the Davises'!"

They arrived at Shanon's house in less than five minutes.

"Here we are!" Shanon cried. "It's the red house with the black roof."

"It really is a great-looking house," said Amy, glancing out the window.

"Thanks," said Shanon. "Dad and Mom just painted it."

"Hey, folks!" Mr. and Mrs. Davis waved at them as they pulled into the driveway. When Shanon slipped out of the car, her parents gave her a big hug. "Glad you could stop by," Mrs. Davis said, shaking Mr. Griffith's hand and smiling at Palmer, Amy, and Gina. "But I know I'm not the one you came to see. Come on, I'll take you to Sally!"

Shanon's parents led them to the kennel. In a cozy back cage, Shanon's dog, Sally, lay with her five pups.

"They're so cute," exclaimed Amy.

"I love them!" cried Palmer. "I wish we could take them back to the dorm!"

"Too bad there's a rule against it," sighed Shanon.

"They really are adorable dogs," Gina said. "I like the way the mother looks, too."

"I've always heard that Jack Russells are a nice breed," said Mr. Griffith.

"Which one would you like to hold?" Mr. Davis asked proudly

Mr. Griffith leaned forward and smiled. "I think I'll take the smallest one," he said, pointing to a brown and white pup.

"Good choice," said Mrs. Davis. "She's the runt, but she's the spunkiest dog in the litter. My husband and I are fond of her, too. We've started calling her Gracie."

Shanon's father gave Gracie to Mr. Griffith and then gave each of the girls a pup to hold.

"Isn't this nice?" Shanon said with a grin. "If only Lisa were here. Hey, I know! Let's take some Polaroids so she won't miss out on seeing Sally's pups."

"Great idea!" said Mr. Davis. "I'll go get my camera!"

After an all too brief visit with the Davises and the dogs, Mr. Griffith and the girls took off for Ardsley.

"Some day, huh?" Palmer sighed, stretching her legs in the back seat.

"Great," agreed Amy. "I just hope I run into John at the game."

"I'm sure Mars will be there," said Shanon. "After all, he's the one who suggested we check out practice today."

"It should be interesting," Gina said from the front seat. "I haven't been to Ardsley that many times. And I like to watch soccer!"

"I hear they have a great team," volunteered Mr. Griffith.

Shanon sighed. "I can't believe that Lisa is missing all of this."

"Well, at least we took the pictures for her," said Amy. "It's too bad we can't bring one of those pups back to school so she can see the real thing."

"Hey, I have an idea," Palmer whispered so Mr. Griffith wouldn't hear. "Maybe we'll be able to bring a pup to Alma after all."

"What do you mean?" asked Shanon.

"I know of a certain couple who need a wedding gift," Palmer said softly. "And fast!"

While Mr. Griffith visited with a colleague, Palmer quickly explained her idea for the perfect wedding gift. Then the girls found seats near the athletic field to watch the soccer team practice.

"I wish Lisa was here," said Shanon.

"I think you've said that a thousand times," Gina said sympathetically.

"Think about something else for a change," Amy suggested.

Palmer pointed across the field. "I think a very cute distraction is headed this way!"

Following Palmer's gaze, Shanon blushed deeply. "It's Mars," she said, taking a breath.

"Oh, my gosh," said Amy, "here comes John!"

The two Unknowns circled the back of the field and made a run for the bleachers.

"Hey, Foxes!" the boys called out.

Amy and Shanon stood up and made room for them.

"Glad you could make it," John said. He turned to Amy's roommate. "Hi, Palmer, nice to see you."

"This is our friend Gina," said Amy.

Gina was shaking hands with John when Palmer suddenly elbowed her in the side.

"Hey, what's the idea?" she asked.

"That's the idea!" Palmer said, pointing excitedly to the field. "Look, Gina! There's Themba!"

Mars leaned forward. "You know Themba Somali? He's one of the best forwards we've got. Check out his style."

Gina sat transfixed as she watched the boy she'd met in the shoe store dart up and down the field. His grace and agility were extraordinary.

"Themba's a great athlete," John volunteered.

"Gina knows him," Palmer announced.

"I do not!" Gina hissed.

"But you want to," Palmer continued. "Gina writes for the newspaper and she wants to meet people from other countries," she explained, turning around in her seat to face the others. "She wants to interview students our age from countries in Asia or Africa."

A burst of applause from the small audience drowned out their conversation. "Why did you say that?" Gina whispered furiously. "What I do is my business!"

Palmer shrugged. "Suit yourself," she whispered. "But I wouldn't be afraid of him just because he's a boy."

Gina blinked. "I'm—I'm not afraid of him," she said.

The team took a break and Mars got up. "Can I show you ladies to the water fountain?" he said, grinning at Shanon.

"Sure," said Shanon shyly. "Then I'll show you some pictures I took of the puppies. . . ."

"We'll go, too," John said, helping Amy up. "If you want me to introduce you to Themba," he added in Gina's direction, "just say so."

"That's okay," Gina said quickly.

"Themba's neat," Mars added. "He gets along well with most of the guys I know."

"Even though he does drive the girls crazy," John said with a chuckle.

"What's that supposed to mean?" Palmer asked, eager to gather information for Gina.

John blushed. "Not much. He just likes to tease girls, that's all. But I'm sure he won't tease Gina if she's writing a serious story."

"Catch you later," Palmer said suddenly. She'd spotted an Ardie she knew. "Get that story," she told Gina before she darted away.

Gina was left all alone on the bleachers, but not for long. To her surprise, heading right in her direction was Themba.

"So what do you think of the team?" Themba said without introduction. He gave her a dazzling smile.

"Great," said Gina, swallowing hard. "I didn't—I didn't know you went to Ardsley."

Themba smiled again. "Greatest school in the world—

don't you think? Even though some of us are thieves."

Gina felt flustered. She remembered what John had said about how Themba liked to tease girls. "I don't understand. . . ."

"I took that thing you had around your neck," the boy said with a laugh. "You left it in the shoe store. I had a feeling I'd run into you again."

"You have my scarf?" she gasped.

"Sorry," he said, bowing his head. "I don't even know your name."

Gina stuck out her hand. "Gina Hawkins. If you want to return the scarf, I live at Fox Hall at Alma."

When he smiled, Gina could see his dimples. "Great." He started to turn away. Gina's heart raced. If she wanted to do a story on him, now was her chance. The material for *The Ledger* issue was due soon. Shanon had already done a lot on her recycling article, and Kate had made headway on her story about the town government. But for all her ambitious ideas about tying in Alma to current events, Gina had come up with a blank.

"Themba—" She stepped off the bleachers. He turned around and looked at her questioningly. Gina wasn't sure what to say next.

"What is it?" he asked.

"Would you mind if I wrote a news story about you?" she asked, blushing. "I mean, you're South African," she blurted out by way of explanation.

"Sure," said Themba dramatically, "I'll tell you all about the jungle!" He laughed and winked at Gina.

Gina frowned. "I don't get it."

"That's what many people think of when they think of Africa," he explained. "I lived in a city," he added as he broke into a run.

"Themba!" the coach barked loudly.

Gina stared after him, feeling bewildered.

Themba laughed and waved his hands in the air. "I'm coming, Coach!"

Palmer crept up next to Gina. "Looks like you two had a long talk," she whispered.

"I'm going to, uh, do a news story on him," Gina stammered.

"I guess you'll be getting to know Themba better," Palmer teased her as they sat down in their seats.

Gina rolled her eyes. "Is that all you think about?"

Palmer gave her a serious look. "Of course not," she replied, "but I think meeting new people is interesting. And if they happen to be boys, why should I hold it against them?"

Gina laughed. "For an air head, you make sense."

"For an intellectual, you're not so bad yourself," Palmer countered as Amy, John, Shanon, and Mars returned from the water fountain.

"So, when's the date, uh, I mean interview?" Palmer whispered.

"Gosh," Gina said, "I don't know."

John leaned forward. "Themba asked me to give you this," he said, handing Gina a brown paper lunch bag.

Gina peered into the bag curiously.

"Show me!" hissed Palmer.

Gina smiled and pulled out a short note. In red pen

Themba had written: "The Ardsley boat house. Three o'clock. Tomorrow!" If she could get permission from Miss Grayson, she might just have her story.

CHAPTER 8

—◆—

Lisa arranged her dolls and stuffed animals on her bed. They were toys she'd been collecting all of her life, but it had been a long time since she'd actually played with them. She picked up Oats, her favorite teddy bear. Oats had been a part of her life before she was born! Her mom had received him as a baby shower gift.

Rubbing the teddy bear's nubby head, she wandered over to her bedroom window. It was Saturday. Her mom was down in the kitchen and her dad was out in the garden. Looking out of her bedroom window, she could see her dad hammering at a fence. The garden of the McGreevy house was usually magnificent, and Lisa was sure that this summer would be no exception. Gardening was only one of the many hobbies that her parents shared. The McGreevys also liked to play golf and tennis and to travel together. In fact, Lisa realized that her parents did most things together. It was hard for Lisa to think of them apart, except when she imagined her dad in his law firm or her mom selling real estate. And to Lisa's great relief, she'd never have to think of her parents as separate. If her mom and dad were getting divorced, there was no way they could have been so loving and patient with her all week. She'd have to talk to Reggie about jumping to conclusions!

"May I come in?" Lisa's mother knocked softly on the door.

"Sure, Mom," Lisa said brightly.

Mrs. McGreevy entered the room. "I see you've straightened up your old dolls," she said. She gave Lisa a wistful smile. "It's hard to believe how time flies."

Lisa nodded. "I think I'll take Oats back to school with me. I want to introduce Shanon to my other best friend." She tweaked the teddy bear's ear.

Mrs. McGreevy sat down on the bed. "I'm glad to see that you're feeling better," she said.

Lisa stared blankly. "Oh, yes, I'm fine now," she said. "My, uh, homesickness is gone."

Her mother's soft brown eyes searched her face. "Dad and I were very surprised to get Miss Grayson's call. She said you had an urgent need to be at home for a few days."

"I did at the time," Lisa said with a grin.

"You haven't told us what the problem is," said her mother.

"Yes, I did," Lisa said, crossing to her dresser. "I told you I was homesick. And now that I've been home for a few days, I'm not anymore."

"And what brought on this case of homesickness?" her mother prodded.

"Nothing," Lisa said. "I mean, I don't know. It just happened. The green dress you bought me is cool," she said, deftly changing the subject. How could she tell her mom that she'd been worried sick by a silly letter from Reggie? Her parents would probably laugh in her face. Or they might get mad at her for taking time off from school for such a silly reason. Besides, the fact that she'd even thought her mom and dad were getting divorced was so embarrassing, Lisa didn't even want to bring it up.

"If you're having trouble with a boy," Mrs. McGreevy said, "you can confide in your father and me. If we didn't think your reasons for coming home were serious, we wouldn't have allowed it. We've tried not to push you, Lisa. We've tried to be patient. We stayed in town because you wanted to come home. Now, the least you can do is—"

"You stayed in town because of me?" Lisa said in surprise. "I'm sorry. Where were you planning to go?"

"Dad has business in San Francisco," her mother replied, "and I. . . ." For a moment her voice trailed off, and she wrung her hands. "I thought a trip would do me good also!" she added brightly. For an instant, Lisa thought that her mother looked upset. But a split second later, Mrs. McGreevy looked fine.

"Come down after you've washed your hands," her mother said, rising abruptly. "Lunch is almost ready. I've fixed your favorite." Giving Lisa a quick kiss, Mrs. McGreevy headed for the staircase.

Lisa ran a brush through her glossy, dark hair. Something about the talk she'd had with her mother seemed kind of strange, as if there was something she was missing. *It's probably because I didn't tell them the real reason about why I came home*, Lisa thought, feeling guilty. But there was no way she was going to bring up the subject of

81

divorce. She might even hurt her parents' feelings by mentioning something so unlikely.

Downstairs, Mr. and Mrs. McGreevy were already seated. At the foot of the stairs, Lisa overheard them talking.

"I distinctly asked you not to go through my mail, Joan," her father complained. "Now it's probably lost somewhere in the house. If you'd get rid of some of this clutter—" Seeing Lisa enter, her father stopped talking.

"Lisa," he said, "I didn't see you. How are you, princess?"

"Okay, I guess," Lisa replied. It was the first time since she'd come home that she'd heard a cross word out of her father's mouth. "Did you lose something, Daddy?" she asked, sitting down at her place.

"Nothing that can't be replaced," said Mr. McGreevy. He cleared his throat and glanced at his wife.

"Your father's going on a trip and I may have lost his itinerary," Mrs. McGreevy explained, passing the sandwiches.

"Oh, are those the plans you had to change because of me?" Lisa asked. "I'm sorry."

"It's not your fault if you have problems," Mr. McGreevy said gently. "After all, our children are the most important thing to us, no matter what happens. . . ."

Lisa frowned. "What do you mean by that?"

"I mean," Mr. McGreevy said, straightening up in his chair, "that we're not letting you go back to that school unless you tell us what's troubling you. When you got here, you looked depressed."

"I was," Lisa confessed, "but like I told Mom, I'm not

82

anymore. Mom told me you were going to San Francisco," she said, trying to change the subject.

"Did she also tell you that she was going to Paris?" Mr. McGreevy asked.

Mrs. McGreevy rose suddenly and tipped over her water glass. "Oh, what a mess," she exclaimed, sopping up the liquid with her napkin. "I didn't tell Lisa about that yet, Dave," she said nervously. "I was going to."

"When?" he asked with his voice rising slightly. "Tomorrow? The next day?"

Lisa's mother began to clear the table and serve dessert. Her father peered over at Lisa.

"We want you to go back to school," he said. "But we're worried. It's not like you to run home because you're homesick. Now, for the last time, tell us what your problem is."

"I really don't have one!" Lisa exclaimed. "You have to believe me! I'm sorry if you canceled your trips. I'm definitely ready to go back to Alma."

"Are you sure, princess?" Mr. McGreevy asked, touching her face gently.

"Honest," Lisa said. "I . . . uh, wouldn't lie about it."

"In that case," Mrs. McGreevy said, "there's a flight tomorrow morning and your dad and I think you should be on it."

"Sure," Lisa said. "I'm not homesick anymore. I told you."

"I hope not," her father said, "because this summer's going to be a bit different. You and Reggie are starting Camp Sycamore earlier."

"Aren't we going to the beach this June, like always?"

83

asked Lisa. She waited for her parents to answer.

Her mom and dad looked at each other.

"We've canceled those plans," Mrs. McGreevy said quietly.

A silence fell over the table. Lisa thought that both of her parents looked nervous. Her father got up without a word and went back to the garden. Her mother disappeared into the kitchen with the dessert dishes.

Left alone at the sunny table, Lisa realized that even though her mother's apple pie was the same, something had definitely changed. Her mother and father were always looking at each other as if they were sending silent messages. Lisa hadn't even noticed it during the first part of the week, but now it dawned on her that her parents might have a secret, too. She wondered what it could be. One thing she knew for sure—whatever was on her mom and dad's mind, it wasn't divorce.

Just then, the postman came up the front walk. Seeing him through the window, Lisa jumped up.

"Anything for me?" she asked, running outside. Maybe Shanon had written again!

"Sure thing, Lisa," the postman said, handing her an oversized envelope.

A big smile broke out on her face when Lisa saw the return address on the orange and blue oversized envelope. It wasn't a package from Shanon; it was from Rob!

"Good news, huh?" the postman guessed.

"You could say that," Lisa said with a blush. Grabbing the rest of the mail, she ran to the porch. Sitting on one of the white wicker chairs near the front door, she tore open the package. Rob's letter was stuck inside a thin gray book. She opened the envelope.

Dear Lisa,

I got your home address from the Alma student directory and sent this letter by overnight mail. I hope you don't mind my writing you at home, but I miss you! Why did you go home? I'm also wondering why you stopped writing to me. Am I going to see you before the end of the school year? Enclosed is a copy of my class book and a self-addressed, stamped envelope. Please sign next to my picture and send the book back. It would also be nice to know if we're going to write over the summer. If you have anything on your mind, please write me about it. You can trust me.

Your friend,
Rob

P.S. I hope you're not home because of your tonsils. (smile)

Lisa smiled and opened the book. Rob's picture was on the third page. Next to it, he had drawn an arrow and written the words "Reserved for Lisa." Warmth flowed through Lisa's body. Rob really cared about her! She grinned at his picture. Though he looked cute, his smile had come out kind of goofy-looking. Lisa leaned back in the big chair and sighed. The friends she'd made at Alma Stephens were good ones, as were the Ardsley boys she'd met. Glancing at Rob's letter again, she laughed out loud at his joke: "I hope you're not home because of your tonsils!" Rob had gone home earlier in the year, too. Lisa had been very worried when she didn't hear from him. At first her only news was that Rob was in the hospital. Fearing he was seriously ill, she'd been greatly relieved to learn that he was only having his tonsils removed. . . .

Lisa sat up in her chair suddenly. "Gosh, I've been ignoring Rob," she said out loud. For weeks she'd avoided writing him. She hadn't even told him that she was going home! Suppose he needed to get in touch with her? Suppose Shanon hadn't told Mars where Lisa was going? In fact, Lisa realized, from the way Rob's letter sounded, he probably wasn't sure if Lisa liked him anymore. And she did like him—more than ever! Not only that, she *did* trust him! She decided to write to him that minute. What a lucky thing it was that she had good news for him. Dashing up the stairs, she pulled open her desk and found some stationery. But her ballpoint pen had run out of ink. She ran down the corridor to her parents' room, but the door was shut. Just as she was about to open it so she could search for a pen, she stopped at the sound of her father's voice on the other side of the door. She hadn't even seen her father go upstairs. He must have come in from the garden through the back doors.

"That's just like you, Joan!" Mr. McGreevy said sharply. "When do you propose to tell the children?"

"Please . . ." Lisa heard her mother say, "you promised!"

"We can't keep them in the dark forever," Mr. McGreevy shouted. "You didn't even tell Lisa about your Paris trip."

"Lisa has problems," Joan McGreevy argued.

"She says she's homesick," countered her husband.

"I don't believe that," Lisa's mom cried. "It has to be

something else that's troubling her. And I'm certainly not going to upset her more than she is already!"

"Don't accuse me of trying to upset Lisa," Mr. McGreevy said. "I've been walking on eggshells all week. But I'm going to San Francisco and that's that! You're not going to stop me, Joan. We've talked this thing through a million times. Now, I suggest that—"

Her mind reeling, Lisa leaned against the door. She didn't want to hear any more! Her parents were fighting, just like Reggie had said! And there was no doubt in Lisa's mind that the argument was serious.

"Let's be honest for a change, Joan!" Mr. McGreevy went on.

"Please lower your voice," Mrs. McGreevy begged. "How can we be honest with the children when we're not even honest with ourselves! I'm so confused, Dave."

Unable to stand it any longer, Lisa raced into her room and slammed the door shut. Throwing herself onto her bed, she grabbed Oats and began to gulp deep breaths of air. Her mind was spinning. What did her parents' argument mean? After a while, she looked out of the window. Her father was back in the garden working as if nothing had happened. Someone knocked on the bedroom door.

"Are you there, Lisa?" Her mother's voice actually sounded cheerful!

Lisa managed to find her voice. "I'm taking a nap," she answered. She sat down at her desk. What could she do? She needed somebody to help her; she felt so confused! She looked at Rob's picture in the open class book on her desk and decided to write him a letter. Groping in her desk drawer, she discovered a pencil. For a long time, she sat still, unable to write. Then the words slowly began to form in her mind. . . .

Dear Rob,

I'm so scared. I think my parents are in big trouble. It was a secret I didn't want to talk about with anybody. I've never felt this sort of pain before. I've been carrying this around for a while now. I didn't want to believe it was true. Then I came home and my parents hid the truth from me, and I realized that I've been shutting you out. I'm so sorry!

Today I finally heard my parents fighting. And I found out they don't want to be honest with me and my brother. Whatever their problem is, they don't want to share it. I don't know what to do. I don't really want to know what they are keeping from me. I think it might be too terrible. If my parents get a divorce, I think I'll—

Lisa put her head down on the desk and wept. Then she took a bath and went downstairs for dinner. Her mom and dad were quiet, but acting normal. Lisa wanted so much to ask them what the matter was, but she couldn't. It was too painful. Having a conversation with her parents about what was really going on would be too frightening! But she had to know! Isn't that what she'd come home for?

She went up to her room as soon as she could. For a long time that night, she stayed up in bed thinking. Then finally, she finished her letter:

I know what to do, Rob. Tomorrow I have to find out what's really wrong, no matter how much it hurts. It's time to find out what secrets they're keeping from me.

Love,
Lisa

Having made up her mind, she felt better. Braving the dark, she clicked off the light and snuggled with Oats. "Please, let everything be all right," she whispered. "Please. . . ."

CHAPTER 9

Having received permission to bike down to the Ardsley campus, Gina pedaled as quickly as she could to the school waterfront where she'd agreed to meet Themba.

"Great day," Themba said, settling onto the ground. "I brought us a picnic."

Gina took a seat on a bench.

"You didn't have to do that," said Gina. "I mean, thanks, but this is just an interview," she added awkwardly. She wasn't all that used to being alone with boys.

Themba opened his knapsack nevertheless and pulled out a container. "I brought something you can't refuse," he insisted, "something I remember eating a lot in South Africa."

Gina leaned over curiously. "What is it?" she asked.

"Carrot and raisin salad," Themba explained, passing a plastic fork and paper plate to her.

Gina smiled and took a nibble. "It's good. Did you make it?"

"No, the cook did," Themba said with a laugh. "She knows how I love it! You eat like a rabbit," he teased her. "Look at me!" He shoveled a huge forkful into his mouth.

Gina fixed her eyes on her notes. She didn't like being compared to a rabbit.

"I really don't know very much about South Africa," she began. "I do read the newspapers and I know that the political situation there is changing rapidly. Everyone I know is hoping that the country's citizens will get the civil rights they deserve. But I'm not sure what I really want to ask you."

"Ask me about myself," Themba suggested. "The article is about me, not South Africa. First of all, I'm five foot nine and I was born in April. And I definitely like my name. It means 'the one to trust.' " He smiled at Gina broadly.

Gina blushed. "Okay, I've got a question for you. Why are you teasing me?"

Themba's face fell. "Sorry," he muttered. "Was I doing that?"

"Yes," Gina replied. "And I hear that you get a kick out of teasing other girls, too."

"Did I tease you when we met in the shoe store?" Themba asked apologetically.

"I don't think so," said Gina, feeling even more uncomfortable now that she'd brought up the subject.

"Good," said Themba with a smile. "I guess I do tease girls, sometimes. I do it to make them laugh. Maybe I'm trying to get people to like me. I took your scarf to get your attention. Here it is, by the way." Thembe pulled Gina's red paisley scarf out of his knapsack and handed it to her.

"Oh, I nearly forgot about it, Themba!" exclaimed Gina. "Thanks so much for remembering to bring it along. I guess I'll have to forgive you for taking it since you were nice enough to agree to this interview. But, Themba, you don't have to tease people. They *do* like you!"

"Not always right away," Themba explained. "You have to admit, I'm different."

Gina shrugged. "I'm different from most of the kids around here, too. At Alma there aren't too many African-Americans."

"Yes, but you *are* an American," Themba said. "I love it here, but in this country I will always be a foreigner."

"I see what you mean," Gina said quietly. "Do you want to go back home?"

"I'd have to think about that," Themba said. "Maybe for a vacation, but it probably would be a difficult place to live. I don't have many worries here," he said, looking around him.

"How long have you lived here?" Gina asked, taking notes.

"Most of my life," said Themba. "My family moved here when I was five."

Gina's face fell. "Then I guess you don't remember much."

"I remember some things," he said firmly.

Gina looked at the paper she was holding. "If you were five years old, you wouldn't have known much about politics."

"Even at five I was asking my parents all kinds of questions," said Themba. "It's impossible to be a young South African and not be aware of politics. Too much is going on

92

over there. And for a person our age. . . ." He looked wistfully at the river. "Going home for vacation should be very interesting."

Gina studied Themba's pensive face. At the moment, it was neither teasing nor playful. She remembered her dad's stories about the civil rights struggle in the States.

"It's sad," she said quietly.

Themba nodded. "Neither of us knows how sad it really is."

CHAPTER 10

"I heard you and Mom fighting yesterday," Lisa announced, facing her father with her hands on her hips.

Dave McGreevy looked surprised. "I'm sorry, princess," he said sadly. "We've been trying to keep our problems under wraps while you've been home."

Lisa pushed down the lid of her suitcase angrily. It took every ounce of nerve she possessed to confront her father, and she wasn't sure if she could go through with it. Her dad got up. "Need help?"

"No thanks," Lisa snapped, "it's loaded with books I've barely looked at." *I have to talk to them*, thought Lisa, remembering the promise she'd made to herself. *I have to learn the truth.*

Her father touched her arm gently. "How much did you hear?"

"Enough to know that you and Mom are keeping something from me and Reggie," Lisa burst out, her eyes welling with tears. "Dad, I hope you're not getting a divorce, because if you are," she continued desperately, "I'll . . . I don't know what I'll do!" Trembling, she faced her father again. "Tell the truth, Dad. Is that what's happening?"

Dave McGreevy glanced toward the door. Lisa's mom had just entered.

"It's true, isn't it?" cried Lisa. "It's not fair! I want to know why!" Along with the hurt she'd been feeling for the past few weeks, there was also deep anger.

Her father grabbed her arms and caught her in a big hug.

"I love you and Reggie more than anything in the world," he said softly.

Lisa pulled away and looked at him accusingly. Her mother was still standing at the door. "More than Mom? She's the one you're supposed to love! And now you're going to San Francisco and making her go somewhere else!"

"That's not true," Mr. McGreevy said quietly.

"No, it isn't," her mother volunteered. "Taking separate trips was my idea."

Lisa sniffed and sat down on the bed. "It was?" she said, blinking away her tears. "I don't understand. . . ."

"It's hard for us to understand, too, princess," said her father, sitting down next to her.

"We've been seeing a marriage counselor," Mrs. McGreevy confided, taking a seat on Lisa's other side.

"Marriage counselor?" Lisa said, feeling even more bewildered. "That's for people who have real problems."

"We do," her father admitted. "And we want you to know they have nothing to do with you."

"I hope not," said Lisa in a trembling voice. She turned to her dad and then looked at her mom. She loved them both so much!

"There's no shame in having problems, Lisa," her mother said, stroking her hand. "But it is wrong to run away from them. That's what your father and I have decided *not* to do."

Lisa sighed. "I don't understand. You're going to Paris, and Dad is—"

"We need space and time to reflect," Mr. McGreevy explained, getting up. "Like a grown-up time-out. Remember the time-outs you had when you were little?"

Lisa smiled weakly. "I had an awful lot of them. But they always made me feel better," she added thoughtfully.

"And that's what your dad and I are trying to do," Mrs. McGreevy said, giving Lisa a pat on the arm. "Spending some time apart is a decision we made during counseling. We have to sort things out."

"Your mom didn't think we should even tell you and your brother about this," volunteered Lisa's dad. "It's a very grown-up situation and we're not quite clear on it yet."

"I'm not clear on it either," Lisa said forlornly. "Are you going to be . . . separated?"

"No," Joan McGreevy replied hastily. She glanced at her husband. "At least we hope not."

Lisa's dad bowed his head. "People change, sweetheart."

"And relationships change," her mother added. "Daddy and I are trying to meet the challenge."

"But you haven't changed," Lisa protested. "At least I don't think so."

"We haven't changed in our feelings toward you," her dad said.

Dave McGreevy stood up and closed Lisa's suitcase for

her. "You sure do have some books in here!" he quipped.

"Not to mention the new dresses we bought," her mother added, forcing a smile.

Lisa got up and paced the room. "Things aren't going to change too much, are they?" she ventured. "I mean, I'm still going to have my room—"

"Of course you'll have your room," Mr. McGreevy assured her. "And I want to make one thing clear—your mom and I are not planning to get a divorce."

"Or even a legal separation," said Mrs. McGreevy. "We're just going through a time when our marriage needs attention. And we're doing all we can. . . ." Her voice trailed off. She and Lisa's dad held hands.

"You still love each other?" Lisa asked helplessly.

"Of course we do!" said her dad.

"And we love you, too," said her mother. "Everything will be all right. You'll see. . . ."

Lisa felt a wave of relief wash over her.

"I guess I was being silly," she said with a nervous chuckle. "I shouldn't have even come home. I should have known that you two weren't going to break up."

Her dad lifted an eyebrow. "That's why you came home?"

"What about your homesickness?" asked Mrs. McGreevy.

"I sort of made that part up," Lisa confessed. "Reggie heard you fighting and . . ."

"Oh, now I get the picture," said Mr. McGreevy.

"This is the last time we keep the kids in the dark," he vowed, turning to his wife.

"You're right," Lisa's mom admitted. "Otherwise they

might imagine that we're worse off than we are."

"You mean there's nothing really serious going on at all?" Lisa said, feeling light-headed. "You mean, you and Mom were just having a little fight yesterday and you're going on separate trips and that's it? There's nothing at all to be worried about?"

"It's a bit more serious than that, honey," Mrs. McGreevy said quietly.

"But we'll get through it," her dad assured her.

Lisa's mom kissed her. "We love you, Lisa. . . ."

All the way to the airport, Lisa was quiet. Her parents didn't say much either. The things they had discussed in her room gave her a lot to think about. In spite of her parents' assurances, she felt very scared. It was as if she and her parents were in a small craft on a big ocean. A feeling of uneasiness stirred in the pit of her stomach. She hoped that her parents had told her the truth—she wanted more than anything in the world to believe that they would never divorce, that her home would stay the same forever.

Kissing her mom and dad good-bye, she climbed on board the plane that would take her to Boston, where she would catch the train to Brighton. The bright spring day and the thought of seeing her friends again sent her spirits soaring in spite of her family problems.

Lisa felt a growing sense of anticipation as her cab approached Fox Hall. In a way, Shanon, Palmer, and Amy were her family, too.

"Lisa! Lisa!" Shanon ran toward her as she entered the common room.

"Shanon!" Lisa cried, dropping her suitcase on the floor and throwing her arms around her friend.

"Hi, Lisa," cried Palmer. She came over and gave Lisa a kiss on the cheek.

"How was it?" Amy asked, mussing Lisa's hair.

Lisa stood back and took a deep breath. Just then, Miss Grayson joined the group. "Hi, there," she said gently. "Is everything okay at home?"

Lisa smiled. "I think so."

"Yaay!" yelled Shanon. "This calls for a celebration!"

"Maybe we should order out for a Monstro from Figaro's," said Amy.

"But first," Palmer reminded them, "we've got to show Lisa the pictures of Sally's puppies."

"Oh, I can't wait to see them!" Lisa squealed. "Let's do it right now."

Shanon pulled a thick envelope out of her bookbag. "Now, this one we call Gracie," she said, picking out a snapshot that looked more like a bundle of brown and white fur than anything else. "She's pretty comical—and rambunctious!"

"She looks like a real ball of fire, all right," Miss Grayson said, laughing. "I've never seen anything so cute in my life. I'd give anything to have her."

Shanon's face lit up. Palmer nudged her and tried to stifle a giggle.

"They're really sweet," Lisa said, looking closely at the photo.

"Mr. Griffith saw them, too," Shanon whispered excitedly to Lisa. "Wait until you hear about our plan."

Suddenly Miss Grayson was at Shanon's elbow. "We'd

99

better let Lisa go to her room so she can rest and unpack," she advised. "She's had a long day."

"We've also got studying to do," Amy said with a groan.

"Okay," said Shanon, picking up Lisa's suitcase to haul it back to their suite.

Palmer led the way down the hall, as if the four of them were a parade celebrating the return of an astronaut from outer space.

"You guys are the best," Lisa declared happily. "I couldn't have hoped for a better homecoming!"

When they were alone in their room, Lisa turned her back and unlocked her suitcase.

"I want to introduce you to a special friend of mine," she said. "Ta-dah!" Lisa turned back around. "Meet Oats!"

Shanon laughed softly. "Is that your teddy bear?"

"Yes," Lisa said, hugging the stuffed animal. "He looked kind of lonely at home, so I thought I'd bring him back with me." Depositing Oats next to her pillow, she plopped down on the bed. "At least things haven't changed around here."

"I'd never change anything without asking you first. Next year, let's get a new poster," Shanon said.

"No," exclaimed Lisa. "I mean, I missed our room. I like it the way it is."

Shanon came over and sat next to Lisa. "Was everything really okay at home?"

"I'm not sure," Lisa confided. "But at least I got my parents to be honest with me." She looked at Shanon. "To tell you the truth, I'm still kind of upset. I don't know what to tell Reggie."

"Tell him exactly what happened," Shanon suggested.

Lisa sighed. "At first everything seemed great, like I said in my letter. Then I heard my parents having a fight. When I finally got up the nerve to ask them about it, they said they were seeing a marriage counselor."

"That's too bad," Shanon said quietly.

Lisa frowned. "I hope it all turns out all right. Of course, nothing like that would ever happen in your house."

"Is that why you waited so long to tell me about Reggie's letter?" Shanon asked.

"I think so," Lisa confessed. "And also . . . you don't like to hear about things that are upsetting."

"That's not true," Shanon protested. "If anything else bad happens to you, I want to know! I'm your best friend. You can trust me."

Lisa smiled. "That's what Rob said. But your family is so different from mine," she said thoughtfully.

"Your mom and dad are wonderful," Shanon said loyally. "And I think anybody in the world can have marriage problems. Just think of all the kids we know whose families—"

Lisa's eyes filled with tears. "I know," she said softly. "I'd be one of them."

Shanon squeezed her roommate's hand. "Maybe you won't be."

"Well, whatever happens, I'm glad to be back," Lisa said, giving her friend a hug.

"I'm glad you're back, also," said Shanon. "And now we have a new roommate," she said, picking up Lisa's teddy bear. "So what do you think, Oats?" she asked. "Should we start studying or go to The Tuck Shop for a shake first?"

101

"Go to The Tuck Shop," Lisa said, imitating a bear's growl.

Shanon laughed and put Oats down. "He's going to be nice to have around." She gathered her notebooks and markers.

"Might as well go to the library afterward," Lisa said, unpacking her books. "I don't even want to think about all the work I'll have to do to catch up."

Before they left Suite 3-D, Shanon and Lisa stuck their heads in the other bedroom and invited their suitemates to come along. Although she felt a little guilty, Shanon was actually pleased when Palmer and Amy both declined. It seemed like such a long time since she and Lisa had been together.

As the girls stepped out of the door, Shanon grabbed Lisa's hand.

"What is it?" Lisa asked.

"You are going to be my roommate again next year, aren't you?" Shanon said in a rush.

"Of course," said Lisa, "you don't have to ask."

"I mean if things go badly with your parents . . . you are coming back?" Shanon ventured.

"I'm coming back no matter what," Lisa declared. "Once a Fox, always a Fox."

"Great," breathed Shanon. "You mentioned before you went home that you might stay."

"That was silly," said Lisa. "No, it's Alma Stephens for the next hundred years of my life," she joked. "Or for as long as you're my roommate," she added, grinning at Shanon.

The two girls took off down the stairs. Shanon crossed her fingers and whispered, "Roommates forever!"

CHAPTER 11

My Picnic with Themba
by Gina Hawkins
When I first got the idea of interviewing Themba Somali for *The Ledger*, I made up a list of questions all about politics. I planned to ask him things like: What was it like growing up in a place where you and your family might be denied basic freedoms? How did it feel to be unable to choose what kind of work you do or where you get to live? How does it feel for your entire family to obey the same curfew rules? Soon after our meeting at the Ardsley riverfront, however, I discovered that Themba didn't have much firsthand knowledge of these issues, since he's lived most of his life in America. But he has seen a great deal

through the eyes of his father, who's
been a well-known actor in New York
for the past twelve years. . . .

Shanon sat up abruptly on the loveseat when she heard
a knock at the door.

"Come in!" she called out, putting down the final issue
of *The Ledger* she'd been reading before the interruption.

"Here's the rest of the money Kate and I collected for the
present," Gina announced, holding out a wad of dollar
bills.

"Great," said Shanon. "Even though my parents aren't
charging us, we want to make sure we have the cost of the
shots covered."

"Not to mention that cute collar we saw," Palmer said,
coming out of her bedroom. She smiled at Gina. "I hope
nobody gave you any flack about our decision. You must
admit—Gracie is an unconventional wedding gift, to say
the least."

Gina shook her head. "Everybody thinks the idea is ex-
cellent, and Muffin checked out the rules thoroughly.
There's nothing on the books about faculty keeping pets."

"Then it's settled," Shanon said, letting out a sigh of
relief. She picked up the newspaper and grinned. "I was
just reading your article about Themba. It's great."

"Thanks," Gina said a bit wistfully. "Themba likes it,
too. I sent him a copy."

"This is my favorite part," Palmer interrupted. She
picked up the paper and leafed to the last paragraph of
Gina's article:

" 'Through honest talks with people our age of different

nationalities and backgrounds, we can find out more about what's going on in the world and have more control over the future of the planet we share. Many young people are not as lucky as those of us at Alma Stephens and Ardsley. Some children are natives of countries torn by war and political unrest. But they are kids just like you and me and Themba Somali.' "

Gina smiled. "I'm glad you liked it. I thought Shanon's recycling article was great, too."

"What did *Themba* think of your article?"

Gina blushed. "He sent me this. Read it for yourself." She pulled a letter out of her pocket.

"I can't believe it," squealed Palmer. "Gina's got a pen pal! I thought you said you weren't interested in writing to boys," she teased.

"I wasn't, I mean, I guess I am now," Gina muttered, looking embarrassed.

"Give her a break," said Shanon sympathetically. "I know how it feels to be teased."

"Okay," Palmer agreed, snatching the letter. "But I'm going to read what Gina's *boyfriend* had to write to her."

"Will you cut it out!" said Gina. "He's not my boy-friend. He's just a friend."

With a knowing smile, Palmer read Themba's letter out loud.

Dear Gina,

I liked the article you wrote. The interview really made me think. I even remembered some things afterward. When I was very little I played in my grandfather's village when I visited him. We used to make toy cars out of wire. I used to imitate my grandfather by putting a blanket over my shoulder and by pretending I was walking with a cane. I don't know why I'm telling you this—the story is finished. I hope I see you again, soon. I promise not to tease you. But it's fun getting a serious person like you to smile.

Your picnic partner,
Themba

P.S. I miss having your scarf in my dorm room. I used it for a lamp shade.

Palmer burst out laughing.

"Themba really is a character," said Shanon.

"He can be a funny guy," Gina admitted. She shook her head. "Using my scarf for a lamp shade. . . ."

"What I like most about him is that he teases you," Palmer declared, "just like I do."

"I like him most when he *doesn't* tease me," said Gina.

Shanon and Palmer glanced at each other.

"So you do admit you like him?" Palmer asked hesitantly.

Gina smiled awkwardly. "I can say this much. Of all the boys I've ever known, I've come the closest to liking Themba."

Shanon looked at her watch. "Oops! We've got to go! Amy and Lisa will be waiting."

"I have to go, too," said Gina. She clutched the letter tightly. "Thanks a lot for listening."

Shanon smiled. "Anytime."

"See you later," said Palmer.

Once Gina was out the door, the two girls disappeared into their bedrooms.

"What's on your schedule this afternoon?" yelled Palmer, grabbing her French vocabulary list and putting on a sun visor.

"I need to do Latin," Shanon yelled back. "Amy and Lisa are studying math." The two girls reappeared at the front door with armfuls of books.

"These study sessions had better pay off," Palmer grumbled.

"Don't worry," said Shanon, "they will. Let's go!"

The two girls jogged across campus to The Tuck Shop. Amy and Lisa were seated at a table for four.

"Sorry we're late," said Shanon.

Lisa smiled. "That's okay. We stopped by Booth."

"Listen," Palmer said, taking a seat, "Shanon said you guys wanted to do math, but could we please start with French first? I'm so behind I—"

Amy stuck out a fistful of envelopes. "We might want to start with these," she said, grinning.

Palmer's eyes lit up. "Letters!" She grabbed the one with Sam's handwriting on it.

Shanon smiled and took the envelope addressed to her. "Maybe we *should* read these first," she said. "Otherwise, we won't be able to keep our minds on studying."

"Sounds good," said Lisa. "I'll go get us some sodas."

While Lisa was placing their order at the counter, Amy showed her letter from John to Shanon and Palmer. "I already read it to Lisa." she explained, "Want to hear?"

"Fire away," said Palmer.

Dear Amy,
If I had to coin a phrase for this year, I'd call it "Here

107

today, gone tomorrow." That's how quickly this year has flown by. I can't believe that next week we're taking finals. Needless to say, it was a dee-light to see you at the soccer practice. I hope we get another chance for a run-dey-voo (that's French for I hope I'll run into you) before the end of the year.

Love,
John

"He's so nice," sighed Shanon as Lisa came back with the sodas.

"Almost as nice as Sam," Palmer said, tearing open her envelope.

Dear Palmer,
What a great coincidence that you were shopping while I was working at Suzy's. I liked your friend Gina. Did she ever find Tim? My face has totally cleared up from the chicken pox—finally! It's a good thing, too, because The Fantasy is performing out of state next weekend. What are you doing this summer? You looked great in that pink dress. Write soon.

Love,
Sam

"Good letter," said Amy. "Now let's hear yours," she said, turning to Lisa.

"No, let Shanon go first," Lisa said. She tapped Shanon's leg beneath the table with the toe of her sneaker. "Come on, don't be shy. . . ."

"I'm not being shy," Shanon protested. She opened the envelope. As she scanned the letter, her face turned a deep shade of pink. "It's kind of personal," she hedged.

"Come on," said Amy.

Shanon took a breath. "Okay, here goes nothing. . . ."

Dear Shanon,

Did I ever tell you that you are the neatest girl I ever met? I liked holding your hand at the soccer match. Please keep writing me this summer!

Mars

"I can't believe how romantic he is!" Palmer sighed.

"He's in love with her," Amy said with a nod.

"No, he's not," Shanon said, her cheeks burning. "I knew I shouldn't have read it out loud!"

"It's okay," Lisa said gently. "They're just teasing you. We all wish our pen pals would write us romantic stuff like that."

Palmer stared at Lisa. "Well, what are you waiting for? Open yours up."

"I haven't heard from Rob in a while," Lisa said. She fingered the envelope nervously. "I wrote him from home that afternoon after I heard my parents arguing."

"So what's he going to do," said Amy, "write you a mean letter because your parents were arguing?"

"No, that's not it," Lisa protested. "It's just that I think I hurt his feelings when I stopped writing him. I also wrote him a pretty personal letter. I hope he didn't think it was embarrassing or anything."

"Only one way to find out," Shanon prodded.

Lisa opened Rob's letter. She read it to herself and then passed it around.

Dear Lisa,

I got your letter. I'm so very sorry that things are not going well in your family! I know how you feel—my mom and dad were separated once. My parents got back together, though, so there was a happy ending. If you ever feel like talking or writing to me about it again, please do. I was worried about you a few weeks ago.

My dorm proctor is taking me to meet his old biology prof—a guy who now teaches at Alma. I'll be there on Sunday the 24th, I think. Maybe I could meet you somewhere, like under the clock. That way you could give me my class book back. John and Mars got to see Amy and Shanon at soccer practice. I want to see my girl, too.

Yours truly,
Rob

"*My girl!*" said Palmer. "Rob's letter is almost more romantic than Mars's."

"He's being really sweet," Lisa admitted bashfully.

"It's too bad you have to give back his class book," said Shanon. "It's been so much fun looking at it."

"Wow," Amy said, "Lisa's really got something to look forward to. She'll actually get a chance to see Rob before school's out. I'm totally jealous."

"The twenty-fourth," Lisa said, beaming.

"Oh, no!" said Shanon. "That's the day of the wedding."

"But the wedding's in the morning," Palmer reminded her. "By the time Rob arrives, it'll be all over and Maggie and Dan will be married!"

Amy clapped her hands together. "It's going to be *so* great."

"I just hope they like their present," said Shanon.

"Sure they will!" Palmer piped up. "How could they *not* like it?"

"Well, it's going to be a big surprise," Shanon said doubtfully. "I hope it's a pleasant one."

"We can't back out now!" Palmer exclaimed.

Lisa pulled out her notes from history class. "We can't back out of this either."

Amy grinned. "She's right, gang! Foxes become grinds at finals time!"

CHAPTER 12

"Am I glad that finals are over!" Amy sang out gleefully. Having darkened her already black lashes, she plunked down the mascara and began to mousse up her hair.

"I thought I'd never get through it," sighed Palmer. "I'm not sure I did," she added, applying a coat of lipstick.

Shanon stood back and admired her peach-colored dress in the mirror. "I hope we're not putting on too much makeup," she said, eyeing her three suitemates.

"Don't worry," Lisa said. "Maggie and Dan's wedding isn't a school function. And I say we should look our absolute best for it." Finishing off her eye makeup with a hint of light green shadow, she tied her gleaming dark hair with a big ribbon.

"If you say so," Shanon said, smiling. "Anyway, I think we all look sensational."

"I think so, too," Palmer said, stepping into blue pumps the same shade as her billowing dress.

Amy buttoned the collar on her green silk blouse and put on a black cinch belt. Lisa grabbed a flowered shawl to wear with her red dress, and Shanon placed a straw hat on her head.

"There," Lisa said. "I think we're ready."

"Should we clean up the suite now or later?" asked Shanon. The room was strewn with skirts, dresses, and blouses that had been tried on and discarded.

"You've got to be kidding," said Amy. "I'm much too excited to do anything now!"

"Don't forget the gift box," Palmer cautioned.

Shanon picked up a big box with a pink ribbon taped to the top and set it down by the door. "Don't worry. This is one thing that's going with me. As soon as my dad brings Gracie over, I'll put her inside. I even made holes in the top so she can breathe during the ceremony."

"Great idea!" said Palmer.

Shanon picked up the box. "Let's go."

The girls made their way across campus. The sky was a cloudless robin's-egg blue, and flowering trees lined every walkway. "It smells delicious out here," Lisa said with a sigh.

"It makes me feel like singing," said Amy.

"Not now, if you don't mind," said Palmer. "I'm too nervous."

Shanon and Lisa laughed. "Nervous?" said Lisa. "How come?"

"Weddings always make me kind of nervous," Palmer confessed. "Of course, I've only been to two—my cousin's and my father's. I'm always scared something might happen to ruin it."

"Like what?" Amy asked curiously.

"Well, the groom might forget the rings, or the bride

might be late, or the flower girl might get nervous and forget to walk down the aisle. That's what happened to me," Palmer admitted. "I was the flower girl in my father's wedding. I was so scared, they couldn't get me to move."

"You can relax," said Amy, giving her a playful pat on the shoulder. "You're not in this wedding, so there's no way you can ruin it."

"Nobody can," Shanon sang out from behind the big box. "This wedding is going to be perfect!"

"When's your dad showing up?" asked Lisa as they approached the Alma Stephens Meeting House.

Shanon put the box down. "He said that he'd be here in time," she replied. "You three go on into the garden. I'll wait for Pop."

"Okay," said Amy. "We'll stand in the back and save a space for you."

Leaving Shanon just outside the Meeting House, Lisa, Palmer, and Amy entered the large formal garden where two musicians were playing classical guitar and flute. Several friends and faculty members had already gathered. Up front on the left, Kate, Muffin, and Gina sat with the Fox Hall contingent. Kate waved when she saw Lisa. "It's all set," Lisa mouthed to her.

Palmer and Amy sat down in a back row.

"I wonder where Maggie is," Lisa whispered, slipping in next to them. The three girls looked around. Maggie Grayson was nowhere in sight, but they did see Dan Griffith. Dressed in a blue blazer and gray flannel pants, Mr. Griffith looked very elegant and serious. The girls recognized the man standing next to him as the town's Unitarian minister. Close by, there was a teenage boy who looked very much like Dan.

"Who's that with Mr. Griffith?" Palmer whispered.

"It's probably his best man," Amy replied.

"He looks an awful lot like Dan," Lisa added. "Maybe it's his brother."

"Whoever he is," said Palmer, "he's dreamy."

Shanon slipped in next to Lisa. "Operation Gracie now under way," she said with a smile.

"Where's the box?" asked Lisa excitedly.

"I put it in front with the other gifts," Shanon whispered. "Behind the big table."

The girls peered at the table Shanon was pointing to. It was on the other side of the garden, behind a rose trellis.

"That's kind of far away," Amy said doubtfully.

"She'll be fine there," Shanon assured her.

Suddenly there was a stir in the congregation. Shanon, Lisa, Amy, and Palmer all turned at once and let out a gasp. At the end of the aisle stood Miss Grayson!

"She's gorgeous," Lisa exclaimed in a whisper.

Palmer nodded. "That dress is so elegant."

"She looks really happy," Amy said, beaming.

Tears filled Shanon's eyes. In her simple, white satin dress and shimmering veil, Miss Grayson was almost too beautiful to be real. The luscious bouquet of pink roses she held added the perfect final touch. The flutist and guitar player shifted into a lilting melody and Miss Grayson began to walk down the aisle.

Shanon squeezed Lisa's hand.

"I know," Lisa whispered. "It's wonderful!" For a fleeting instant she thought of her parents. She knew from the wedding album she'd seen at home that her mother had been just as beautiful at her wedding as Maggie was now. As Maggie walked past them, holding her head high, Lisa blinked back her tears. Her teacher's beaming face banished all thoughts of sadness.

The couple faced the minister beneath a rose trellis. "I hope the box is okay," whispered Amy.

Shanon nodded, straining to hear the minister's words.

"Seriously, you guys, I'm worried about Gracie. Puppies don't know how to behave at weddings," Amy continued.

"Shhh!" hissed Palmer. "You're making more noise than the dog! Will you relax?"

The girls were transfixed when Dan slid the ring on Maggie's finger. Suddenly someone tittered.

"What's so funny?" Lisa wondered aloud. "This part of the ceremony seems pretty serious to me."

In the back row, the girls heard a wave of hushed conversation from up front.

Shanon craned her neck and leaned forward. "I don't know what's going on up there. I can't see."

Suddenly a loud bark pierced the silence. A chorus of laughter followed.

"Oh, my gosh!" Shanon gasped.

Lisa groaned. "This is a nightmare."

"I hate to say 'I told you so,' but we shouldn't have left the box alone up there!" Amy said nervously.

Too shocked to move, Shanon and Lisa watched as Gracie put on a show in the aisle. First she nipped at the hem of Maggie's gown, and then the frisky puppy got a firm grip on one of Dan's cuffs. A white bow almost as big as

116

her body was tied around her new collar. From a distance, the little brown and white dog looked like an unidentified flying present. But her excited yipping left no doubt as to what Gracie really was. Mr. Griffith finally loosened the puppy's grip from his cuff and held her up for the whole crowd to see.

"What a comedian," Palmer said, laughing.

"How can you laugh?" Amy said, shutting her eyes. "We've ruined the wedding."

"Maybe not," said Lisa, thinking quickly. Squeezing past Shanon, she calmly walked up front.

"Excuse me," she said, taking Gracie from Mr. Griffith. "I think we have a crasher." She gave Dan and Maggie an apologetic smile. "Gracie wasn't supposed to make her appearance until the reception."

Mr. Griffith smiled broadly. "It's okay. No harm done."

"But please show her to the garden for now," Maggie added, her eyes twinkling. She rubbed the puppy's head. "See you later, Gracie!"

There was a sprinkling of applause in the crowd as Lisa slipped down the aisle carrying Gracie. She headed right for the garden, with Shanon following.

"I've never been so mortified in my life," Shanon said, barely able to breathe.

"They took it well, though," Lisa said. "I don't think we ruined the wedding."

"I saw Miss Pryn's face," Shanon added in a worried voice. "Imagine, letting a dog loose at a wedding! It's all my fault. I should have—"

"Relax," said Lisa. She put Gracie down on the ground. The dog began to race around. "Look at her go."

117

"I wish I had that much energy," said Shanon.

"Maggie really likes her," Lisa said. "I could tell by her face. And so does Dan."

"Want to go back inside?" Shanon asked. "I can watch Gracie. No sense in us both missing the rest of the wedding. Unless it reminds you."

"Of my parents?" said Lisa. "It did for a minute. But now I feel okay. Thanks for asking, Shanon," she said gratefully. She gave her roommate a quick kiss. "You're a great friend. This summer I'll really miss you."

Lisa joined Amy and Palmer for the close of the wedding ceremony, while Shanon and Gracie stayed outside in the garden. Afterward, the girls headed for the reception line to greet the couple. Miss Pryn came up to Shanon, who was holding the puppy.

"Quite a show-off," the headmistress said with a gleam in her eye.

"Yes, ma'am," Shanon gulped. She tried to restrain the squirming puppy. "We checked the rules," she said bravely, "there isn't one against faculty having pets . . . is there?"

Miss Pryn shook her head. "Not to my knowledge. And I should know."

Shanon breathed a sigh of relief as Miss Pryn walked to the head of the line.

"I think old Prune likes Gracie," Amy said mischievously.

"She's one person I'm not going to miss this summer," said Palmer.

"I think her bark is worse than her bite," said Lisa.

Gracie yipped. "See," Lisa said with a laugh, "even Gracie agrees."

When the four suitemates neared the front of the reception line, they were joined by Gina, Muffin, and Kate.

"It was a fiasco up there with the dog," Kate said, shaking her head.

"I couldn't believe it," Gina said with a chuckle. "I was just about to get Gracie myself when Lisa saved the day."

"Quick thinking, Lisa," Muffin piped up.

Palmer touched Gina's arm. "How are things going? Did you answer Themba's letter? Did he write you back?"

Gina smiled wistfully. "I did write to him. And I got a letter back from him. I think it'll be a long time until I ever see him again, though."

"Why?" asked Shanon curiously.

Gina sighed. "I'll show you the letter later. . . ."

Having reached Dan and Maggie at last, the girls shook hands shyly with their newly married teachers.

"I'm glad Gracie could come to my wedding," Maggie laughed, giving each one of the girls a kiss. Dan hugged them all, including Gracie.

"She's a feisty little thing," he said with a grin.

"I hope we didn't ruin your wedding," said Palmer.

"Of course not," said Maggie. "Nothing like a little excitement to spice things up."

"We should have known," Dan added, "that the Foxes of the Third Dimension were behind it."

Shanon blushed and held on tight to the wriggling puppy. "Gracie is a gift from all of us at Fox Hall," she explained. "There is a card on top of the big box behind

119

the gift table, the box where Gracie was supposed to stay until *after* the ceremony!"

Maggie beamed with gratitude. "I'm speechless. . . ."

"Well, I'm not," said Dan. "It's the best gift we could have gotten. Only do us a favor . . ." he added with a wink, "baby-sit for Gracie until the reception is over?"

"Sure thing!" said Shanon.

"Wow," said Amy, looking toward the far end of the garden, where a band was tuning up next to a portable dance floor. "There's going to be live music!"

"I'm going to take Gracie back to the dorm before the party starts," said Shanon excitedly.

"I'll go with you," said Palmer. "These new shoes are squeezing my toes. I've got to change."

Shanon turned to Lisa. "What about you?"

"I'll stay here for a while. As long as you're going back, will you bring Rob's class book for me?"

"You bet," said Shanon.

Palmer turned away. "I'd give anything to see Sam O'Leary today."

"I wish I was seeing John," said Amy.

Lisa lowered her dark eyes and smiled. At least for today, the pain she'd felt for the past few weeks had vanished.

Leaving the reception early, Lisa walked across campus and stood by the big clock. In her arms she clutched Rob's class book as she waited for him to appear. Her heart pounded as she saw her tall, dark-haired pen pal ambling toward her with another young man.

"This is Irv," Rob said, introducing his dorm proctor.

"Hi," the other boy said with a smile. "Catch you in a few minutes, Williams," he said. Soon Irv was out of sight.

Lisa smiled. It seemed as if a hundred years had passed since she'd seen Rob. "I have your book," she said softly.

"Thanks." Rob's deep blue eyes darted to her face. "Did you, uh, have time to sign it?"

"Oh, yes," Lisa said, leafing through the pages. "Sorry I didn't mail it back." Rob came and stood beside her, brushing against her shoulder.

"You look great," he said.

"I got dressed up for the wedding," Lisa said, stealing a glance at his handsome profile.

Rob's face lit up when he saw what Lisa had written beneath his picture: "To R.W., my pen pal and a real friend. From L.M. Forever!"

"Forever, huh?" said Rob, smiling broadly. "Does that mean this summer?"

"Yes," said Lisa. "I'll be in camp. But I can still write!"

"Did Rob say anything about Mars?" Shanon asked later that evening. The four suitemates were sitting out on the stoop of Fox Hall.

"Mars and John have already left for home," Lisa replied.

"I thought so," sighed Shanon.

"I got a note from John yesterday with his home address," Amy said happily.

"I already know Sam's home address," Palmer said. "I just have to make sure he has mine. I hope he writes me."

"He will," Lisa assured her. "Sam's crazy about you."

Palmer tossed her head and grinned. "I think so, too. Sam's my fav rave forever."

"That's not the way it seemed at the reception," Shanon teased. "Anybody would think that your fav rave was Dan Griffith's brother."

All the girls laughed, including Palmer.

"What's the joke?" Gina asked, joining them on the stoop.

"Nothing," Palmer said, blushing. "Did you bring the letter from Themba?"

"Yes," said Gina. "When I sent him that letter I showed you, he'd already left. Luckily, Ardsley forwarded it. This is what he wrote back."

Shanon took the thin piece of air mail stationery, covered with Themba's neat handwriting.

Dear Gina,

I am writing to you because I didn't get a chance to say good-bye. I left school a little sooner than I planned because we took an earlier flight to South Africa. . . .

"South Africa?" Palmer squeaked.

"His family was planning to go for a vacation this summer," Gina explained, "but now. . . ."

"Let me finish," said Shanon.

My dad has been offered the directorship of a very exciting theater project. This means that I will not be coming back to Ardsley. I didn't know it when we had our interview, but my family and I are finally going home, maybe for good. I'm not sure how I feel about it. I hate to leave my school and all my friends.

Good-bye if I don't see you again soon.

Love,
Themba

Shanon's eyes misted over. "That's a great letter! But it's also sort of sad."

"Themba's a special person," Gina said proudly. "I'm definitely going to keep up with him." She smiled at Palmer. "Even though he is a boy, I won't hold it against him. Will you write to me this summer, too?"

"Sure," Palmer said with a grin. "We'll exchange addresses later."

"We should go in," Amy said after Gina went back inside the dorm.

"I've got so much packing to do," Palmer muttered, staring at the twilight sky.

"I never thought I'd say this," Shanon said softly, "but I don't want to go home." She glanced at Lisa, who smiled back.

"We're all going to be together again next year, aren't we?" Palmer burst out.

"Sure we are," Amy said, squeezing her shoulder.

"Hey . . ." Lisa said with a hint of mischief in her voice, "let's have a sandwich."

Everyone stood up and hugged. "See you next year!" Amy said with a giggle.

"Don't get too sunburned." Palmer laughed.

"I'll send you all postcards from camp," Lisa said with

a grunt. "It's called Camp Sycamore, but we call it Camp Sick More, because of the food!"

"Oh, no," groaned Shanon. "You'll wish you were here with Mrs. Butter."

The girls huddled even closer, then laughed and jumped up with their arms outstretched. "We've made it through our first year!" Amy cried out.

CHAPTER 13

———◆———

Dear Sam,

Just to let you know that I'm at home. You can write me now! My mom has been sweet. I think she missed me. We are going on a cruise with my aunt in a couple of weeks. I will send you a postcard. I never thought I would miss Brighton, but I do. It's kind of boring here. Well, I have to go! Good-bye for now!

Yours truly,
Palmer

Dear Palmer,

I keep trying to imagine where you live, but I have never been to Florida. It must be hot! The Fantasy and I have been picking up more gigs. We are performing in another state competition next week. On top of that, I got a job at Figaro's delivering pizzas. I quit Suzy's. I'm real sorry that I didn't get to see you again before you left for home. Next year I'm going out for football. Will you come to some of the games? I'm glad that you're interested in meeting my friends. I'm even more glad (gladder?) that we're writing. Have fun on the cruise! Think about me a lot.

Yours,
Sam

Dear Themba,

What a surprise to learn that you are home in South Africa! Though we knew each other for only a short while, I'm very glad that we met this year. I was wondering, could we be pen pals? Whether you like this idea or not, please write to me and let me know how you are. I hope you like it there. It is hard for me to imagine what your country is like, since I've never been there. Also, there are a lot of scary stories about South Africa in the newspaper. My dad and mom read the article I wrote about you in The Ledger and they were very proud of me. They were also interested in hearing about your father because they have heard of him. Write soon.

Yours sincerely,
Gina

P.S. My friends thought it was funny that you used my scarf as a lampshade.

Dear Gina,

I got your letter! And I'm happy to report that I'm very, very glad to be home. Yesterday I went on a hike with my sister in the mountains. We saw beautiful views of the bay and sparkling beaches. We saw a baboon also! There were twelve mountain peaks in the distance as well, stretching down to turquoise water. We also saw in the distance the island where political prisoners are kept. My sister and I thought it was grim.

My grandparents were happy to see us. They had a big feast in their village in our honor. My parents and I live in a small house in Cape Town township. My father is especially excited to be back, and he's already involved in his project. I didn't think I would like it here. I was also scared by the newspaper stories. I did not realize how much of an American I had become. But now that I'm back, I'm so proud to be a South African. Not only because my country is beautiful, but because I am here at a historic moment! It does not always feel safe, but my father is very good at explaining politics to me. Change fills the air and I feel that my family and I are part of a great struggle. When civil rights come to all South Africans, we will be here! And I would love to have a pretty American girl as a pen pal, especially one with big feet like my sister. (I can't help teasing people I like!) Write soon!

Love,
Your "pen pal"
Themba

Dear John,

New York in summer is hot and I mean sizzling! Last Saturday, my brother took me to a humongous concert in Central Park. It was great to see him again. I think you would like him. His dream is to own a motorcycle, but my dad won't let him. He's going to get his driver's license, though. I'm taking a course in pottery. I'm also taking photography and modern dance. My mother wanted me to take violin, but I said no. Enough is enough. How's your

127

poetry? How's your music? I find it hard to compose here. Too much is going on. But I'm listening to a lot of CDs and old records. My brother has turned me on to Chuck Berry. Check it out! Next month we're going to Hong Kong. Write soon!

Sincerely yours,
Amy

Dear Amy,

You are busy. Me, too. My father got me a job in his law office as a messenger. We may be coming to New York one weekend. I'll call you if we do. Chuck Berry is the greatest—I agree. I'm not into writing music much without you here. But I am reading a lot of poetry, like T. S. Eliot. I definitely believe that my fate is to be a poet. You are the only person who knows this. I didn't see you all that much at school, but I miss you. Have fun in Hong Kong.

Your pen pal,
John

Dear Mars,

I am at home now. Working at the gas pump is fun! We kept two of Sally's puppies for ourselves. I named mine Dan, in honor of Dan Griffith. He and Maggie really liked Gracie, the puppy we gave them. My sister, Doreen, named her dog Shanon as a joke! I hope she finds another name soon! Maybe it is an honor. What do you think?

Life is very strange not being at school. Figaro's is practically deserted without all the kids from Alma and Ardsley. The summer will pass before we know it, I bet! Happy

Birthday! (Surprised that I remembered?) You are getting to be old! (smile) Tell me what kind of cake you had.

Your friend always,
Shanon

Dear Shanon,

I think it is an honor to have a dog named after you. I named my parrot, Ricardo, after a friend I have at home. I have been having bad luck. I thought I would have a summer job as a camp counselor, but it fell through at the last minute. It's too bad, because I like making my own money. I am having a pretty nice time with my friends, though I keep thinking about you. I remember the first time we met—you were at the Halloween party dressed as an astronaut. I finally tried the s'mores recipe. They came out great.

Mars

P.S. Thanks for remembering my birthday. My parents took a bunch of us to a concert. I wish I could have invited you. My cake was coconut.

Dear Rob,

I was only at home a short time before Reggie and I left for camp. The food is definitely sickening, except for the nights when we cook out. Then it is exceptional! I love roasted hotdogs and marshmallows. I also like singing around the campfire. In the morning we are up at sunrise, however. This is hard for me. I go horseback riding, swimming, and rowing every day. I am training for my lifeguard certificate. Reggie isn't good at sports, so he spends most of his time doing computer games. When Mom and Dad drove us here, they seemed happy. There hasn't been any more talk about separating. Mom had a good time in Paris and brought me some perfume and a neat pair of earrings. I don't know about Dad's time in San Francisco. My mother is taking another trip to see her sister while I am at camp. My grandmother is fine. I visited her. I am keeping my fingers crossed about my parents' problems. I try very hard not to think about it. Thanks for being my pen pal this year. You're really important to me!

Love,
Lisa

Dear Lisa,

 I think about you a lot. Try not to worry about your parents. My dad has gotten me another neat summer job from one of his friends. Unfortunately, it isn't in Alaska as I'd hoped or in Pennsylvania (which is a bummer, because I might have been able to see you). Instead, it is on a dude ranch in Arizona. I'll write you when I get there. I like you.

"Forever,"
Rob

Dear Lisa,

 Just to say that I enjoyed being your roommate this year and look forward to living with you again. Do you think we will be in Suite 3-D? I hope so. Do you think we should keep our code name? I say: Foxes of the Third Dimension, forever! Oops! Mom is calling me for dinner. Dan is biting my ankle. He's my new dog. Ouch! Got to run! I have a lot to tell you, but will have to finish this later. I got a letter from Mars! I wish I could read it to you! Have you heard *from Rob? Yikes! Now my dad is calling. You are the best! I hope you are fine and everything's perfect! I miss you a lot. . . .*

(I am finishing this after supper. My puppy, Dan, is asleep on my bed. He is so cute.) It's hard for me to remember what I was going to write before I went downstairs to eat my mother's spaghetti and meatballs (which was great, by the way). I guess I was just thinking about all the amazing things that happened to us this year. Remember the first time we all got together and were bragging about our "dates"? Our dates that nobody ever even had? And then you came up with the idea of advertising for boy pen pals! And what a super idea it was! Just think, I wouldn't have met Mars—and now he is one of my best friends! Remember when we met The Unknown at the Halloween mixer? You liked Rob right away, remember? And then you and Rob ended up acting in the spring play that Gina wrote, and Amy got to play the lead. All three of you were fantastic!

I was also thinking about how we had a fight that time when we were both running for dorm Student Council rep. I guess neither one of us will ever forget that. I'm really glad that we made up! And who can forget the trip to London when Amy sang in the restaurant and Dan caught us sneaking out of the theater. I hope we go on another exciting trip next year. All and all, it has been an all-round "rad" (as Amy would say) year, which I, for one, would not trade for anything!

I wouldn't even trade Palmer in for another suitemate. Even though I never thought I'd get used to her, I have. And I like her, too. And I love Amy. It will be nice to have

Maggie and Dan both living in our dorm. I hope they use the quilt we gave them at Maggie's shower. And I especially hope they love Gracie.

Lisa, I don't think I can write anymore. My hand is tired. But there is just one more thing I have to say and I hope it doesn't sound corny. You are my best friend and I love you.

Signing off from Brighton, New Hampshire,
Your friend forever,
Shanon Davis

Something to write home about . . .

another new Pen Pals story!

In Book Thirteen, Shanon is in for a shock! As Shanon, Palmer, and Amy wait for Lisa to arrive, a tall, red-haired girl walks into Suite 3-D and introduces herself as Max Schloss, their new roommate! Though Max's chauffeur piles more and more luggage into the suite, the girls are convinced there must be some mistake. But is there?

Here's a scene form Pen Pals #13: LISA, WE MISS YOU

"Welcome to Alma Stephens," Shanon said politely. "Want us to help you find your room?"

"Sure," said Max, standing up. She reached into her jean pocket. "This is the room assignment they gave me over the telephone." She showed Shanon the piece of paper. Written on it was *Suite 3-D, Fox Hall.*

"You must have not heard the right thing over the phone," Shanon said. "This is a mistake."

Max's chauffeur brought in a CD player and a trombone case.

"Set the CD player down on the table, Ollie," said Max.

"Very well, miss," said the chauffeur. "I'll leave your trombone case over here by the door."

Max smiled. "Thanks for everything! See you at Thanksgiving!"

"I think we'd better find your room in a hurry," Shanon said, giggling nervously. Max's stuff was taking over the whole suite. "I wonder who your roommate is, anyway."

"Who's yours?" Max asked innocently.

Shanon smiled confidently. "Lisa McGreevy."

"We've had it arranged since last spring," volunteered Amy.

"Unless," Palmer exclaimed, "things got mixed up."

Shanon's face flushed. "Mixed up?" she said. "That's ridiculous. Lisa is my roommate and that's that." She glanced at Max. "No offense, but it was planned."

"That's okay," said the girl, glancing away. She looked at the slip of paper. "But where? . . . ."

Shanon marched to the door. "I'll go find out for you."

In a matter of seconds, Shanon was standing outside Maggie and Dan's basement apartment. There certainly did seem to be some kind of mix-up. Max Schloss had been assigned to their suite. And there had been no sign of Lisa. *Well they'll just have to straighten things out!* Shanon thought. Shanon was supposed to be rooming with Lisa, not with some stranger!

When Maggie opened the door, a small puppy dashed out.

"Not so fast, young lady!" the teacher cried, grabbing

the puppy. She stood up to greet Shanon. "Hi, there! What do you think of Gracie? Isn't she just cuter than ever?"

"Cuter than ever," Shanon said with a swallow. "I . . . uh, there's a person upstairs in the suite," she said.

Dan Griffith stepped up behind Maggie. "What person are you talking about?"

"There's been a mix-up," she explained. "There's someone else who says she lives in the suite and it isn't Lisa."

Maggie touched her arm. "There isn't a mix-up."

"What do you mean?" Shanon cried. "Lisa and I have been planning this. We put in for our assignments. You told us—you can't make me live with someone else," she insisted.

"It's a four-person suite," Dan said. "We have to."

"But Lisa is my roommate," blurted out Shanon.

"I'm sorry, Shanon," Maggie siad. "I guess you haven't heard."

Shanon blinked. "Heard what?"

"It was a last-minute decision on the part of the Mc-Greevys," Dan explained. "We just found out ourselves. Lisa's not coming back."

Shanon's lip began to tremble. She felt as if she was going to cry. "There must be a mistake," she said. "Lisa wrote to me."

"There's no mistake," Maggie said gently. "That girl upstairs is your new roommate."

Where is Lisa? And how will Shanon survive a whole school year living with a total stranger?

P.S. Have you missed any Pen Pals? Catch up now!

PEN PALS #1: BOYS WANTED!

Suitemates Lisa, Shanon, Amy, and Palmer love the Alma Stephens School for Girls. There's only one problem—no boys! So the girls put an ad in the newspaper of the nearby Ardsley Academy for Boys asking for male pen pals.

PEN PALS #2: TOO CUTE FOR WORDS

Palmer, the rich girl from Florida, has never been one for playing by the rules. So when she wants Amy's pen pal, Simmie, instead of her own, she simply takes him.

PEN PALS #3: P.S. FORGET IT!

Palmer is out to prove that her pen pal is the best—and her suitemate Lisa's is a jerk. When Lisa receives strange letters and a mysterious prank gift, it looks as if Palmer may be right. But does she have to be so smug about it?

PEN PALS #4: NO CREEPS NEED APPLY

Palmer takes up tennis so she can play in the Alma-Ardsley tennis tournament with her pen pal, Simmie Randolph III. But when Palmer finds herself playing *against*—not *with*—her super-competitive pen pal, she realizes that winning the game could mean losing *him*!

PEN PALS #5: SAM THE SHAM

Palmer has a new pen pal. His name is Sam O'Leary, and he seems absolutely perfect! Palmer is walking on air. She can't think or talk about anything but Sam—even when she's supposed to be tutoring Gabby, a third-grader from town. Palmer thinks it's a drag, until she realizes just how much she means to little Gabby. And just in time, too—she needs something to distract her from her own problems when it appears that there *is* no Sam O'Leary at Ardsley.

PEN PALS #6: AMY'S SONG

The Alma Stephens School is buzzing with excitement— the girls are going to London! Amy is most excited of all. She and her pen pal John have written a song together, and one of the Ardsley boys has arranged for her to sing it in a London club. Amy and her suitemates plot and scheme to get out from under the watchful eye of their chaperone, but it's harder than they thought it would be. It looks as if Amy will never get her big break!

PEN PALS #7: HANDLE WITH CARE

Shanon is tired of standing in Lisa's shadow. She wants to be thought of as her own person. So she decides to run for Student Council representative—against Lisa!

PEN PALS #8: SEALED WITH A KISS

When the Ardsley and Alma drama departments join forces to produce a rock musical, Lisa and Amy audition just for fun. Lisa lands a place in the chorus, but Amy gets a leading role. Lisa can't help feeling a little jealous, especially when her pen pal Rob also gets a leading role—opposite Amy.

PEN PALS #9: STOLEN PEN PALS

Shanon, Lisa, Amy, and Palmer have been very happy with their pen pals—but now they have competition! Four very preppy—and very pretty—girls from Brier Hall have advertised for Ardsley pen pals. And pen pals they get—including Rob, Mars, and John!

PEN PALS #10: PALMER AT YOUR SERVICE

Palmer's broke! Because of her low grades her parents have cut her allowance. Now she needs to find ways to make money and fast! The Foxes put their heads together to help Palmer with quick money-making schemes *and* to help her with her grades. But they can't do it all. Palmer has to help herself. But will snobby Palmer be able to handle a waitress job?

PEN PALS # 11: ROOMMATE TROUBLE

Lisa rearranges the suite so that all four girls sleep together in the sitting room. And when shy Muffin Talbot